Wit, Wisdom & MisAdventure

Wit, Wisdom & MisAdventure

Personal Triumph Over Murphy's Law

Richard W. Nelson

Warren, Taylor Publications • Dallas

Copyright © 2003, Warren Taylor Publications

All rights reserved. No part of this publication may be reproduced through Photostat copy, xerography, facsimile, microfilm, microfiche or any other means without prior written permission from the publisher. No part of this publication may be stored in any type of retrieval system, or transmitted by electronic, mechanical, photocopying, recording, or otherwise, without the prior written permission of the publisher.

Except in the United States of America, this book is sold subject to the condition that it shall not, by way of trade or otherwise, be lent, resold, hired out, or otherwise circulated without the publisher's prior consent in any form of binding or cover other than that in which it is published and without similar condition including this condition being imposed on the subsequent purchaser.

ISBN: 0-9653865-3-8

Library of Congress Catalog Card Number: 2002092807

Any inquiries or requests for permission to use materials should be directed to Warren, Taylor Publications.

Printed in the United States of America.

For Carrie and Christian

"Security is mostly superstition. It does not exist in nature, nor do the children of men as a whole experience it. Avoiding danger is no safer in the long run than outright exposure. Life is either a daring adventure, or nothing. To keep our faces toward change and behave like free spirits in the presence of fate is strength undefeatable."

- Helen Keller

Acknowledgements

First I wish to memorialize my eternal thanks to Carrie, my wife, and Christian, our son. Their encouragement and support allowed me to pursue many adventures and their love spurred me to return and tell my tale. My dear wife, Carrie Nelson suffered through numerous drafts and revisions.

I would like to thank those who patiently listened to the repeated telling of my stories and for their encouragement.

Insightful comments from my proofreader and editor, Leslie Runnels proved invaluable. Susanne Mailloux and Aaron Watson provided thorough reviews at critical stages of the book's progression. Of course, I'm sure it will be evident where I failed to take their sage advice.

While I will surely fail to list everyone, I would like to thank the people who actually participated in these adventures, those who suffered through my endless storytelling, and those who encouraged me to write this book: Dannielle & Brian Agena, Diane Albiero, Daniel Alessio, Vince Azarro, Don Bascue, Beata & Ian Bodnoff, Mike Buhler, Ulises Corvalán, Robert & Linda Cook, Robert Cross, Burke Duncan, John Entwhistle, Sylvia Forest, Jim Gudjonson, Michele Haines, Marcia Heath, Irma Horne, Kendrick Hughes, Chris Keele, Tammy Keele, Deanne Kimura-Asamoto, Russell Kleman, Kathy & Brian Matise, Grant Meekins, Alexandre Miello, Rita & Dave Minor, Karen Moody, Roy & Thui Nelson, Robin Oliphant, Michael Olsthoorn, Bob Painter, Peter Purcell, Terry Potter, Nancy Silvestrini, Bonnie Streeter, Aaron Watson, and Patricia Woods.

In remembrance of family and friends who have passed away, these are people who have truly affected my life in a good way: Alice Bibo, Herbert Bibo, Lori Bibo, Flora Chavez, Irma & James Horne, Willard & Margaret Nelson;

Walter & Margaret Nelson, Geno Burnell, Lee Foster, Steve Hoschied, Lenny Lemiere, Kenny Lucier, and Marty May. They may be gone but they are not forgotten.

Contents

Mountain Man   *3*

Snowmobiling   *12*

Grandpa   *17*

Pray Daily for a Vacation   *21*

The Cabin   *24*

The Price of Copper   *33*

Skiing   *37*

Boxing   *41*

Marriage   *46*

Cycling In Snake Country   *53*

Polo   *59*

Hobnobbing In Hollywood   *72*

A New Life   *76*

An Introduction To Mountaineering   *83*

Mt. Shafer: Youth is wasted on the young   *94*

Father and Son Camping   *99*

The Tortoise and the Hare   *109*

Mt. Fuller: A hunk of cheese…   *113*

Mt. Fay: Married with Children   *118*

Contents

Ice Climbing   *125*

Avalanche   *132*

Friendship   *141*

Because It's There   *147*

High Altitude – A Lesson in Morality & Leadership   *152*

Aconcagua: Hubris and Humility   *158*

Intestinal Fortitude   *168*

Flying   *180*

Guardian Angels   *186*

Risk Management   *193*

Kings and Princes   *201*

Camp   *206*

Bolivia: A Hungry Animal Hunts   *210*

Introduction

The stories you are about to read are true. In some cases, names have been changed to protect the innocent, not so innocent, and completely guilty. In some cases I have used real names so all can know the guilty parties.

In telling my stories over the past several years, my friends and co-workers had encouraged me to write a book about my experiences. While I'm not quite sure if their encouragement results from their enjoyment of the stories or if it were some kind of ploy to draw my attention so they could escape before hearing any more of them.

The stories are assembled chronologically. Believing that all things happen for a reason I try to learn a lesson, or find the moral, with each new life experience however ambiguous it might be. To that end I have attempted to impart my experiences in humorous fashion, however vague and warped that might be.

As a child I was thoroughly engaged by the stories of my grandparents. Each loved to tell stories and had different but unique approaches at keeping our attention.

My grandmother (father's side) spoke of our ancestry. She often described the people and places of her youth and how people lived in those days. There were fascinating stories of family coming from England on the *Mary and Margaret*, a settlement ship following the Mayflower. There were stories of old west Montana - the birth of the state's constitution and the first governor. She told how her father, a doctor, was paid with chickens and would travel 200 miles to deliver a baby or tend to the sick. As with all families, we had our black sheep too. Although ours happened to be Texas lawyers.

My grandfather (mother's side) was the foreman at one of the largest ranches in Montana. He brazenly stretched the truth to create fantastic stories about life on the ranch and hunting in the mountains. My favorite photograph is of him leading a long pack train of horses into the mountains of Montana during a hunting trip. He is the closest I ever got to a real mountain man. For living such a hard life he was a gentle and kind man, by the time I met him anyway. Ever the practical joker, grandpa always enjoyed getting one over on family and friends. My son, Christian, seems to have acquired that particular gene and exercises it regularly.

My grandmother (mother's side) is still a shining light in my life. At 98, I consider her saintly and devoutly religious, I depend on her daily prayers to keep me safe and healthy. Based on the miracles in her life, I truly believe her to be my guardian angel. By the end of this book, I'm sure you'll agree.

Living, literally, at the edge of a wilderness area in southwestern Montana I was afforded the opportunity to experience the richness of life. From the time I was old enough to open the latch on the backyard gate I spent most of my waking hours in the mountains. My friends and I fished and built enough cabins and forts in the mountains to house the nation's homeless.

Since getting married, my wife has fueled my adventures, coming up with one crazy idea after another. Whenever she begins a sentence with, "Wouldn't it be neat to..." another adventure is sure to follow. After being together over 20 years, it's a trap that repeatedly catches me. I am convinced she must have taken out some large life insurance policy on me.

While English is my first and only language, my

wife and editors have encouraged me to write in a different manner than I speak. Even though I have spent an increasing amount of time in South America, I have not picked up much of that language either. My wife speaks fluent Spanish yet lacks the requisite patience to teach me. Thus I am left to struggle haphazardly.

While possibly suffering from cerebral edema, brain swelling that can lead to death, being able to actually communicate with my Spanish-speaking doctor might have helped. Instead, I was prescribed medicines used for intestinal ailments. While women accuse men of having their brain in their pants, this could very well be the first time a medical doctor reached the same conclusion.

I've enjoyed incredible opportunities to participate in adventurous sports such as boxing, polo, skiing, rock climbing, ice climbing, and mountaineering. The down side has been that I've been pronounced dead, broken way too many bones - some more than once, been bitten by a rattlesnake, and stalked by a bear. To all that I have only one thing to say, helicopter evacuations are the way to go.

Tragedies around the world have given me a new appreciation for life, to see things for what they are, and to find humor wherever it lay. Before judging the cup as half-empty, I now think about whether I'm drinking or filling. Drinking heartily from the cup of life may leave it half-empty sometimes but that just gives me the room to top it off and warm it up.

George Leigh Mallory, the famous Everest mountaineer once said, "What we get from this adventure is just sheer joy. We do not live to eat and make money; we eat and make money to be able to enjoy life. That is what life means and what life is for."

Wit,
Wisdom &
MisAdventure

Mountain Man

I was raised in a small mining town of 9,000 in southwestern Montana. Actually, we lived a couple miles outside of town in a long narrow valley. The row of houses we lived in bordered a huge wilderness area at our backyard fence. By the time I was 6-years-old I would fly out the door at the crack of dawn and make abbreviated refueling landings at home base only for lunch and supper, returning just before dusk. This was a time when powdered milk was our source of calcium, Tang was the food of astronauts and you could leave your doors unlocked.

Living at the edge of a wilderness area, I always was careful to be home well before dark. I never lost sight of the fact that the wild might not want to stay in the wilderness and what better time to escape than in the cover of darkness. Being on the edge of the wilderness it only seemed reasonable that I was the one thing that stood between the wilderness and, well, not-the-wilderness.

I wouldn't say that I was afraid of the dark. I was. But I would never say it.

If my friends and I happened to be caught off guard by dusk there was a panic that would dump gallons of adrenaline into our bloodstream and send us rocketing through the woods to home. Our feet would scarcely touch the ground as leaves and small pebbles whooshed into the air in our wake. Our tenni-runners, as we called our sneakers in those days, would be smoldering from the friction and glowing bright red.

Our tenni-runners often smoldered, usually caused by our small sweaty feet being encased in rubber without benefit of ventilation. Once our feet would get sweaty, there was no way to remove those shoes as the sweat acted like super glue. In fact, I once heard that super-glue actually is a diluted form of foot sweat derived from 8-year-olds forced to wear vintage tenni-runners in a factory in some third world country. For some reason tenni-runners made my feet really dirty even though I had very good hygienic standards - taking a bath almost every Sunday night.

The only footwear worse than tenni-runners was my winter boots, handed down since the dawn of time. They were green un-insulated rubber boots that leaked. It didn't help that they continued to grow at a rate that outpaced me. I would put on every pair of sweat socks that I owned and stuff the front of the boots with tissue paper from an old clothing pattern. It didn't seem to help that the type of rubber used in these particular boots quickly radiated any heat from my feet. The inside of my boots would generally be at least 20 degrees colder than the outside air temperature.

I hated those boots and the fashion statement they made. Within minutes of walking outside my feet would be numb and that worked out fairly well, because I could then focus on trying to keep my hands warm in those knitted gloves that weren't knit very tightly.

After playing out in the snow for several hours it was very painful to go home. Usually the only reason that I would decide to go home is that I had to go to the bathroom and my fingers were too numb to unzip my pants. I would race home and beat my arm against the door until someone opened up and then rush into the bathroom, all the while yelling for my mom to help. When a guy has to go really, really bad and has no feeling in his fingers, there is no time for inhibitions.

At every opportunity my friends and I had we would build cabins out of Aspen trees felled by hatchets that had been pilfered from our fathers workbenches. My father had a wooden keg full of nails and we would regularly fill plastic half gallon ice cream buckets with them to nail the Aspen logs together. We got pretty good at building cabins because they would fall apart shortly after we got them built. That wasn't too much of a concern until we branched out into high-rise condos perched in the branches of very tall Aspens. By the time I was 13, we had even begun adding cardboard to line the floors and walls to keep out the wind. We even got so ambitious as to build toilet facilities but never got it right and left the toilet seat hanging on the wall above the hole in the floor. Invariably though someone was always falling through the hole and hitting the ground ten feet below. We figured that ten feet would put us out of reach of bears and Bigfoot, our two unseen but always present adversaries.

We became proficient in building simple structures such as lean-tos. However, since they are only temporary emergency type structures, we never had much use for them. Looking back, it seems the lean-tos outlasted our cabins by several generations.

As time passed, my parents became increasingly intrigued by my adventures. Every day before I would leave, as we were sitting at the breakfast table, they would question me ad-nauseam about what I'd be doing during the day, how I'd be doing it and who I'd be with. They seemed intent on making sure I had new experiences too. They seemed to have a list and would tell me that they didn't want me playing near the creek, catching wild animals or building anything. As their list grew, it became harder and harder to keep coming up with new and innovative activities.

Their interest in the details of my life came with an increasing number of restrictions too that seemed somehow correlated to the dwindling supply of nails and the declining number of my dad's tools. Whenever my dad lost a tool, I'd not be allowed to use some other tool. It would have been better for all concerned if he could have just taken better care of his tools.

I always longed to be out in the wild untamed wilderness. All I needed was to invent some kind of night light type thingy. I saw Robert Redford play Jeremiah Johnson on TV and knew that was the life for me. Living off the land like he did, even the snow and cold didn't seem to bother him too much. I decided that my goal in life was to become a mountain man.

Given my planned avocation, I didn't have much use for school. Those feelings were underscored by the time I reached seven. Second grade hadn't been much fun the previous year and I wasn't looking forward to repeating it yet again. I resisted as best I could but the institutionalized practices of "the system" finally broke me and I began to learn stuff, as distasteful as it was. It wasn't long before I was able to bend this education to suit my own desires. I decided to learn to read in order to figure out what plants were edible. I went to the library on a regular basis, at least once a month or so, to get books on plants. My hero soon became Eule Gibbons. He was popular during the 1960's and 1970's for his knowledge of edible plants and such. He knew just about everything there was to know about finding plants for food and medicine. It was rumored that he could even eat a pine tree.

What a man!

Not too much later, having fully matured, I had to seriously reconsider his hero status after he started doing cereal commercials on TV. I had accidentally tried the cereal he was pitching one time when I was staying with my grandparents. It was like eating grains of sand, except harder and with less taste.

There were these old people who lived on our street who had their yard full of rabbits and chickens, hundreds of them running freely. One summer, when I was ten, my friend Chris and I had been playing in the woods behind their house and came across a bunch of rabbits. We chased them until one-by-one we caught them. There were probably 15 of them that we caught. We built makeshift cages in Chris's playhouse. In no time at all we had the whole playhouse full of rabbit cages. We used the grass clippings from our yard and vegetables pilfered from our mom's gardens to feed them.

One day, not long after acquiring a few more rabbits, a police car pulled in to Chris's driveway. The policemen came over to the playhouse and asked us where we had gotten all the rabbits. We would point to a rabbit and thoroughly explain how we caught it. We may have been a little excited because it took us only a few minutes to cover the stories for all the rabbits. It might have gone a little smoother if both Chris and I hadn't been taking at the same time, about different rabbits.

After hearing us out, the policeman put us in the back seat of his cruiser. There was a big dark stain on the seat and both Chris and I scooted way over to the side. We supposed that some hardened criminal, probably an axe murderer, was executed right there in the policeman's car where he was caged like a rat. The door and window handles didn't work from the inside. We were trapped like caged animals and we were really scared. We waited for what seemed like an eternity. When the policemen returned he took Chris into their house. When the policeman again returned, he asked me for my name and address. I briefly thought about giving him an alias until I glanced at the dark stain on the car seat. When we pulled up into our driveway, he made me wait in the backseat until he had spoken with my mom. He came out to the police car along with my mom and I overheard him say something about me being a juvenile and I really got mad that he would suggest such a thing. I didn't know what a juvenile was, but it sure sounded awful. Even though I had no idea what I'd done wrong, I knew I was in big trouble.

I was under house arrest until we could go to the Justice of the Peace on Monday. It was Friday and I would have to endure a whole weekend of not knowing my fate.

Would I become another number in the prison system?

Would I really have to break big rocks into small rocks for the rest of my life?

My mom and dad really let me have it. They said I had gone into those old people's yard and stolen their rabbits. How could those old people lie like that?

If I had known about moral outrage I would have had a bunch of it, that's for sure. As it was, I was convicted of the crime by the old people, the police and my parents, which seemed really unfair since Chris and I were the only ones who knew what happened.

I had easily aged four years by the time Monday rolled around. I had never, in my young life, spent so much time indoors. The thought still makes me shudder. I stood patiently glued to my mom as she called the Justice of the Peace. My attempts at coaching her to tell the judge my side of the story only seemed to aggravate the situation, yet I persisted. After all, my permanent record was at stake and I didn't want to be labeled as a criminal for the rest of my life.

Within a few minutes my mom hung-up the telephone. She was hesitant about telling me what the judge had said and I braced myself for the worst. For some reason, Mom waited a long time before telling me that the judge dropped the case against me. Of course I received a lecture about how I should be grateful and that I'd learned a valuable lesson. Since I was convinced that a conviction meant hard labor breaking rocks at the state penitentiary, I was very grateful. Although, having never been a good student, I had no idea what lesson I had learned.

As a free man the air smelled sweeter and the sun shined more brightly that day. The shackles of justice had worn me to the quick and I couldn't bring myself to venture outside our backyard for at least a couple of minutes.

Throughout my childhood it seemed that my dream of becoming a mountain man was constantly being tainted. I loved all the cute and cuddly animals and knew that a real mountain man would have to be able to kill and skin and cook them. I thought it would only be fair that if I somehow managed to catch a wild animal either my mom or dad should do the dirty work, well out of my sight. My mother and father were steadfastly against such barbaric practices. To them, meat came in nicely wrapped cellophane packages at the supermarket. When the nightly discussion came up about letting me hunt, it was clear I had won but my parents refused to move from their stubborn position.

After some time they became less and less able to support their stand and often resorted to statements like "I said no," and, "We'll have no further discussion on this subject."

Luckily, I knew their tactics well and would counter with, "But Dad hunted with grandpa when he was a kid and all Mom's relatives hunt." This cut too close to home and too often pushed them over the edge.

When we were visiting my parents this last Thanksgiving, the subject of hunting came up again. They still hadn't budged one bit. But, I'm getting closer. When I was 16 they made a critical error and told me that I could go hunting when I became 44-years-old.

Ha! I'm finally closing in on being able to fulfill my dream and they won't even see it coming.

My parents allowed me to join the Junior NRA when I was 13-years-old. Once a week we would meet in the basement of my elementary school and shoot 22 rifles at paper targets. On my first day, one of the instructors took me aside and showed me how to hold a gun in the various positions - standing, kneeling, sitting, prone - and to look through the gun sites. When I finally got to fire the gun it was an exhilarating experience. We weren't allowed to use the bullet clip and had to manually feed each round into the chamber. At the end of that first day the instructor gave me the 10" X 10" sheet of targets and told me how close I'd come to actually hitting the paper. I was hooked.

Within a few weeks, and several hundred rounds of ammunition, I had reached the level of Marksman. Upon returning home that night with my certificate of authenticity, I proudly proclaimed myself a crack shot. The very next day I applied for a job as a conservation officer from an ad that was in an *Outdoor Life* magazine. That ad sat right next to one selling land in western Canada for $50 an acre. I know because I clipped it out and am still saving up my money so I can by an acre.

When I was 14-years-old, my parents begrudgingly allowed me to attend hunter safety training. We had to read a book on safe gun practices and then watch a bunch of 8mm movies that were the hunter's version of "scared straight." Luckily the scenes showing guys with bullet holes and body parts blown off by their best friends who mistook them for a deer were in black and white. Even so, there were a few times that I had to sneak off to the bathroom for a cold compress to try and stop my body from shaking so badly. I couldn't eat for three weeks, which was actually good since, at the time, I was a wrestler in school and needed to make weight.

As I approached high school and its educational distractions - mainly girls - I lost sight of my goal of becoming a mountain man. I somehow changed and began to focus on different aspects of life to pursue.

I never did get to become a mountain man. First it was college, then work, marriage and a family. I don't regret the path that my life has taken even one bit. Even though I've moved a few times since my childhood, I am still patiently waiting to hear back on the status of my employment application as a conservation officer. While I know the government isn't very efficient, it shouldn't take 27 years to process my application.

Snowmobiling

One winter when I was about 10-years-old my father bought a used Evinrude snowmobile. It was big and it was heavy. Every now and then we would load the snowmobile into the back of our pick up truck and drive the 25 miles or so west to our cabin on the lake. I never quite understood why we needed to go all the way out to the lake to snowmobile since we already lived in a rural area. But we did it.

The old log cabin had been built in stages beginning in the 1920's and began its existence as a hunting camp. When my father turned 13, his uncles chipped-in and bought him a beat up old car and a book on electrical wiring. My father drove out to the cabin armed with miles of extension cords and proceeded to wire the cabin for electricity. My father still tells stories of how he would take my uncle Walter's Scottish Terrier and use it for running wires underneath the cabin. It seems to me that most of my father's time was spent underneath the cabin unwinding the dog from around the supports holding up the cabin.

Later, his uncles had him felling trees and building additions to the cabin. Luckily, as my father continued working on the cabin he became more proficient and skilled in construction.

By the time I came onto the scene, 25 years later, he was still working on the cabin. Thankfully the wiring had all been replaced and the cabin was mostly complete. The cabin didn't have a furnace or a fireplace for warmth, which are really necessary for all but a few weeks out of the year.

The biggest inconvenience though was the lack of an indoor bathroom. We still had to use an outhouse. This was never a problem as long as the sun was shining but at night it was a different matter altogether. The cabin was so far out in the boonies that even under a full moon it is pitch black outside. At dusk bats could be seen flying at treetop level around any clearing in the trees. Bears would often roam around the cabin sites looking for their own version of fast food. Without fail, no matter how many times I'd go to the bathroom before it got dark I'd still have to get up in the middle of the night. At night the outhouse would somehow move further away from the cabin. It seemed to be a nocturnal building that would frolic around the forest at night, only returning at sunrise. I would turn on every light at the front of the cabin but could only make it to the top front porch step before complete darkness overtook me.

When we'd go to the cabin during the winter the road was only paved to within a couple miles of our cabin. The snow piled along the roadway would be several times higher than our truck. We'd park along the edge of the narrow road and my father would make several trips to ferry all my family members on a toboggan.

Every time we went to the cabin the temperature was –25 degrees or colder, and this was back before we knew anything about wind-chill. As usual we would have to dig down to find the roof of our two-story cabin. By the time my dad, mom, brother and older sister had dug down to the front door, my younger sister and I would look like little gnomes as we sat frozen on the snowmobile.

Once inside the cabin my mom would turn the oven to broil and we would crowd around, propping our feet on the open door so our socks would dry. You see, I had to wear four pairs of cotton sweat socks inside my green un-insulated rubber boots. Since the boots had a hole in them I would cover my feet in plastic bags secured by rubber bands that also served to hold up my socks since they had long ago lost their elasticity. I sat and watched the steam rise from my socks, waiting for my feet to explode into cinders from the heat.

Since the rest of my body was still frozen solid I couldn't flip to broil some other body part. After we were all thawed out from getting to and into the cabin, it would be time to go snowmobiling.

On one occasion my brother Roy had invited a friend, Ken, to come with us. My older sister Kathy had control of the snowmobile and drove up and down the unplowed roads pulling us along on a toboggan. Usually one of us would be dragged along behind the snowmobile keeping a death grip on someone or something still attached to the toboggan while Kathy laughed and had a great time. Ken, thinking he was smarter than the rest of us, hooked his left foot in a rope handle that ran along the sides of the toboggan. Not to be outdone, Kathy maneuvered the snowmobile outside its safe operating parameters, careening out of control at every opportunity until Ken fell off. In retaliation for holding on so long Kathy drug his flailing body for at least another 20 minutes. His screams and cries were drowned out by Kathy's laughter and the chainsaw-like buzz of the snowmobile. By the time she stopped, Ken looked as if he was trying to gnaw his leg off in order to get away. His eyes were glazed over with the haunted look of an animal caught in a steel trap. For reasons no one could figure out, Ken never went snowmobiling with us again after that incident.

The cabin was situated on a small lake and when it froze offered a level and wide-open place to really open up the throttle on the snowmobile and "burn out the carbon" as my father would say. Oftentimes the lake would be covered in a deep blanket of snow.

With my unending fear of water I didn't much like driving out on the lake, always thinking that the snowmobile would plummet through the ice with my little gnome butt still frozen to the seat. My father, in attempting to help me overcome my fear, would use every opportunity to take me out onto the lake.

One weekend, at the beginning of winter, my father had taken my younger sister and I out for a ride. The snow was very deep, at least several feet. I sat on the end, facing backwards, while my sister, Tamara, sat behind my father. As we drove along I was amazed at seeing the treetops poke out from the tracks of the snowmobile. In later life I learned that there are instabilities in the snow around trees. Known as tree wells, snow collects in the branches and doesn't pack down. If you walk, ski, or say drive a snowmobile too close to a tree you could fall down into the well. Getting out of a tree well, lined with soft sugary snow, is next to impossible and archeologists will probably discover your remains several eons after the next ice age. My father must have passed a little too close to a tree well because in an instant we dropped into a big hole and his leg became pinned between the snowmobile and the tree trunk. All of us dug furiously until my father was able to free his leg and somehow we were able to drive out of the hole. As soon as I was able to breath again, I asked dad if he would take me back to the cabin. He told me that we were going to take a quick drive around the lake to "blow out the carbon" and then we would go warm up.

We approached the lake along the side of our boat dock, at least I thought that the little bump in the snow was our boat dock. As we drove out onto the lake I yelled to my father that water was coming up through the snowmobile tracks. He told me to shut up because I was scaring my sister. I did as I was told and benignly sat there, watching the water seep through the tracks as we drove out onto the lake. As we passed the end of the boat dock the snowmobile, in one fell swoop, dropped into the lake with all three of us attached to it.

In a way I felt instantly vindicated and immediately told my dad, "See? I told you so." I can't really verbalize the look he gave me. Perhaps my remark and it's timing could have been better, but hey, he was the one who started it.

The lake is only a few feet deep until you get about ten feet from the end of the boat dock where the depth increases to about 25 feet. Luckily we hadn't made it too far out. We each climbed out of the slushy lake and made our way to the cabin as quickly as possible.

I was too young to help, as my father, mother, brother and sister spent the rest of the day trying to get the snowmobile out of the lake. We went home that night with it still firmly stuck in the slushy mess. The next day they all drove out to the lake and worked all day to free the snowmobile. They had to get someone to plow the road to the entrance of the driveway and then dig a path all the way to the lake in order to get the truck down to the lakeshore. They then had to winch the snowmobile out and into the truck. They arrived home late in the night, well after my sister and I had gone to bed.

The very next weekend my mother and father drove the 28 miles to Butte with the snowmobile still loaded in the truck. On their return the snowmobile was gone and in its place was a camper. My father explained that we had progressed beyond the confines of what the snowmobile offered and that we had become a camping family, but only during the summer.

As for the cabin, that very next spring my father installed a furnace, a fireplace and running water. For some reason my father delayed installing an indoor bathroom. Whenever I'd ask when he was going to build a bathroom, which would happen every night at sundown when we were staying at the cabin, he'd just smile at me without saying a word.

Grandpa

Some Grandpas are remembered as the patriarch of the family or as a profound source of knowledge and history. Other Grandpa's, like mine, can be practical and pretty useful but they are often a handful and need careful supervision. My Grandfather, James, on my mother's side was a ranch foreman and an honest to goodness cowboy. He also was a practical joker.

Every now and then we would go out to the ranch and stay with my grandparents. Whenever we would visit, my grandpa would grab each of us kids in turn and squeeze until our lungs were thoroughly flat, at which point he would kiss us and rub his rough two-day growth of whiskers all over our faces. By the time he would let us go, we would be completely exhausted from trying to fight him off.

Grandpa would take me around the ranch in search of treasures. He would get an old empty gunny sack that once held animal feed and we would spend hours together filling it with booty. Grandpa wore an old sweat stained and dirty cowboy hat. I absolutely loved to wear it while we traipsed around the ranch. There were bent horseshoes, rusty horseshoe nails, bits of rope, the odd piece of barbwire and just about any old odds-and-ends that can be found on a working ranch. Rather than having stuffed animal heads on our walls, we had horseshoe coat racks that my dad had welded together hanging every few feet apart in my bedroom and in the garage. When I was old enough I started searching for saddles, bridles, ponies and the errant 410 shotgun that we might possibly stumble upon out in the barnyard. I was convinced that a pony would fit perfectly in our backyard and during the winter it could share my bedroom.

On one occasion when I was about 7-years-old, grandpa told me that I could have a lamb, if I could catch it. My prior experience with lambs consisted of bedtime stories and the one time I dressed in a lamb costume for a church play when I was five. After roundly begging for several hours, my mom drove me along the dirt road until we came across the herd of sheep that was being moved across the ranch by a man on horseback. Mom stopped the car and we both got out. We walked toward the sheep as they walked towards us. When I spotted several young lambs together I raced towards them. In that same instant something must have spooked the whole herd of sheep because they panicked and ran in all directions. As I ran behind them, the stampeding sheep ran straight at, under and around the sheepherder, causing the horse to panic and rear back.

The sheepherder rode over to my mom and I somehow felt that I was going to be in trouble. While no one said anything, we got into the car and drove back to the ranch, empty handed.

One morning when I was ten years old, grandpa took me with him on his morning chores. We hiked over to the chicken coop where I was told to remain outside while grandpa retrieved the eggs from the infuriated hens. Next we made our way over to the barn where grandpa milked a cow. In no time at all we were on our way back to the house with a bucket full of eggs and one full of milk.

In the rear of the house there was a screened porch that contained this big machine sitting on a countertop. When I asked grandpa if he was going to put the eggs in that machine he chuckled and said, "No, this is a milk separator." He then asked me if I thought there was milk inside the eggs. I mustered my best indignation for a retort, which at the time was no more than a sheepish, "No" while scrunching my shoulders and scratching at the dirt on the porch with the toe of my sneaker. As soon as we got inside the house grandpa made a point of telling everyone there, about 30 relatives, that I thought milk came from chicken's eggs.

Most times when we would visit, Grandpa would have someone chase down a horse for us to ride. This involved having an adult chase the horses either on horseback or in a truck until they wore it out enough to catch it. The kids were only allowed to ride Split Ears or Danny Boy, which had belonged to my mother when she was a young girl. Once captured, the horse would be saddled. The stirrups were removed so that, in the likely event we fell off, the horse wouldn't drag us around the ranch hanging upside down from a stirrup.

Being just a kid, horseback riding meant sitting on the back of a horse while it meandered around the front yard of my grandparents' house eating grass. The horse's girth seemed to grow in proportion to its age and my legs would be splayed out, barely reaching the sides of the saddle. Even though I would be tightly holding onto the reigns, the horse would stretch its neck and rip them right out of my hands.

One summer my older sister and brother got to stay with grandpa and grandma for a few weeks during summer vacation. One day my parents received a call from the hospital that my brother, Roy, had an accident resulting in a compound fracture of his wrist. There are conflicting versions of exactly what had transpired. Roy says that he was riding Danny Boy when the horse started bucking violently, throwing him to the ground and stepping on his wrist. My sister, Kathy, says that Roy was standing in the saddle trying to do circus tricks when he slipped and fell off. Even with the passage of many years, both hold fast to their stories. I'm not sure if it was because of my reputation or Danny Boy's but for some reason I was never allowed a turn at staying with my grandparents.

On my grandparents 50th wedding anniversary all of the immediate family showed up for the event. There were about 200 people in the basement of the local church. My grandfather, dressed in a suit and tie for one of the very few times during his life, donned a rubber mask of an old man. It was rather odd to see my grandfather, an old man in his own right, wearing a mask depicting an old man. He wandered around the festivities, scaring the children and annoying the adults. It was a catered affair, which for us meant that everyone cooked a dish. One of my uncles had butchered a couple pigs and brought cured ham. Unfortunately the ham hadn't fully been cured from whatever ailed it to begin with and everyone who ate it got food poisoning, which was pretty funny since I hadn't eaten any.

After all those years my grandpa did leave a lasting impression on me. Since my son was old enough to appreciate it, several times a day you would be able to hear a familiar screech followed by, "Mom, Dad's rubbing his picky's all over my face again."

Pray Daily for a Vacation

As a 5-year-old, I would regularly make the rounds throughout our neighborhood knocking on doors and looking for friends for myself, as well as for my brother, sisters and parents. Once I hit the mother-lode, another family with five kids all in a similar age range to our family.

The Minors were a close-knit family and a fun loving bunch. After a particularly brutal strike at "The Company" they moved to Seattle where Dave, the father, found work at a steel mill and Rita, the mother, became a banker. Each summer they would come to visit for vacation and stay at our mountain cabin for two weeks. It was a time of great anticipation that I relish even in my distant memories. I would always have my clothes and the sleeping bag packed up weeks in advance of their arrival, wholly expecting their invitation to spend vacation with my best friend, Brad.

One year both our families agreed to meet in Canada and spend a week vacationing together. The Minors rented a travel trailer to pull behind their nine-passenger station wagon and traveled through British Columbia on their way to Banff in Alberta. We loaded up our self-contained (meaning it had a bathroom) truck camper and headed due north from our home in Montana.

Having a much shorter trip, we arrived in Banff a few days prior to the Minors. As I milled about the campground, I employed my usual past time of looking for "stuff." Having such a broad definition was helpful because anything that I came across was exactly what I was searching for.

As a young child I was always a little closer to the ground than my friends. I wasn't short, mind you, just a little closer to the ground that's all. Being close to the ground allowed me to get a better view of nature and was instrumental in finding stuff. Finding a lot of stuff is reason enough why someone would want to stay close to the ground their whole life.

Some people can look their entire life and not find anything of value. I, on the other hand, could find worldly treasures just about any place. Canada was no exception. The campground opened its pine needle covered floor to reveal a truly magnificent heirloom. It was something that would guide me through life.

I found a small medallion which had the words "Pray Daily For A Vocation." Of course, being the worldly man that I was at eight, and never having seen such a word as "Vocation" before, I automatically assumed there was some kind of misprint and that the medallion really said "Pray Daily For A Vacation." This seemed much more to my liking and certainly worthy of a daily prayer. I believed that carrying this medallion meant that I would be blessed with many vacations. This medallion was better than fame, fortune or even magic. It signified the utmost in happiness. I promptly tied my new medallion on a string and hung it around my neck proudly displaying my treasure and newfound philosophy.

The adults and older siblings in our little clan spent the balance of our vacation trying to tell me that Avocation means a job. They would regularly poke fun and make me the butt of their jokes. But alas, I would have no part of their buffoonery. They were jealous of my medallion and were somehow trying to take it away from me.

I've later run across the word "vocation" and have not taken much of a liking to it, especially when my name is used in conjunction with it. Initially I heard it from my parents. Oh, they wouldn't dare say the word, knowing my aversion to it but they would get their point across.

My loving wife, never wanting to be left out of anything, has occasionally couched her sentiments by asking me, "What do you want to do when you grow up?"

I'm never quite sure where she's coming from sometimes. There have been a few occasions in my life when I've prayed daily for a vocation but never while rubbing my medallion. That's probably why I've never gotten a really good vocation.

Everyone needs to have a basic philosophy to help them get through every day life. Praying daily for a vacation is not only a philosophy but is a spiritual direction. It transcends any one religion. The bible pretty much spells it out for us. When God created the earth, what did he do on the seventh day? He took a vacation! Don't you suppose that's what he was praying for on the previous six days?

Perhaps all the debate in Congress about school prayer would be alleviated if it were focused around a specific topic. What religion or civil liberties group would be opposed to praying for a vacation? Everyone can use a vacation.

I don't know about you, but when I think vacation, my mind goes to a happy place. Can you imagine, if we are all praying for a vacation there would be no more stress. People would wait their turn in lines. Everyone would drive the same speed on the freeway. People would say, "Please" and "Thank You." New Yorkers would stop being rude. The world would become a utopia.

Still, after thirty-something years, anytime Mrs. Minor talks to my parents she still inquires about my medallion.

Well, she can't have it.

I still pray daily for a vacation.

It's good to have a goal in life.

The Cabin

My sister, a year younger than I, was a member a church related club during middle school and high school. As far as I could ever tell, this was some far out fanatical religious group with a penchant for bake sales.

One year, when in high school, Tamara was elected as queen. To celebrate, all the girls in the group had a pajama breakfast at our house one Saturday morning. Normally, I would make my self scarce at any type of social gathering that included my sister. As luck would have it, I had nowhere to run.

As the only male in this group of 14 females, I was able to work my charm and quickly became the center of attention. There was one particular person in the group who caught my attention. Lori was the outgoing queen and at 21 she was a full-fledged older woman. I instantly became smitten.

At first, Lori seemed coy with me, completely ignoring me, but I could see right through her facade. Not to mention that I could almost see right through her pajama top. Not that I was looking or anything.

Lori baited me and tested my resolve by feigning an interest in my 21-year-old brother who was home on a break from college. I'm sure it had nothing to do with him being a star athlete and a pre-med student. He was still asleep and Lori continually volunteered to go and wake him.

My mother was wise to her ploy and told her it wouldn't be a good idea, especially since he only slept in his underwear. This bit of information only seemed to fuel Lori's interest. I knew she was only feigning interest in him to see if I was jealous. Female gamesmanship! If she only knew that I was not to be outsmarted.

Being a 16-year-old red-blooded male is a unique stage in life. Thank heaven we only have to experience it once. It is an especially unique experience if you're in Montana where the population of actual human beings is limited, let alone the female variety. Any gathering of women in pajamas must be taken with all seriousness, after all, it could be a once in a lifetime phenomenon. Not that being a 16-year-old virgin and thrown in with a group of women - at least one dominant older women - dressed in a short frilly nightgown could have any underlying meaning.

While my mother and father had always told me, usually around report card time, that I could do anything I wanted if only I applied myself, I never was able to apply the philosophy to any practical life event. Until then. Being so near a sexy older woman dressed in pajamas seemed to provide an epiphany. I was beginning to see what my parents were trying to get across to me. All this time I had thought their lectures concerned my lack of educational initiative. Instead, they could see that their youngest son was in fact far beyond his years and in need of more refined tutoring through life's difficulties. Gee, are moms and dads smart or what!

Lori happened to work as a restaurant hostess at a resort hotel ten miles east of town. My friends and I recreated at this resort frequently on weekends. Actually, the only time we weren't there was when the high-handed security guards caught us doing something they felt was not fully appropriate. Mind you, we never did anything illegal. Maybe a little questionable. Anyway, I sought Lori out at every opportunity on the weekends to flirt with her.

During these romantic interludes, in front of the hostess station, I would jokingly bring up the subject of dating and eventually gathered the courage to ask her out on a date. Though suave and debonair, I tried not to overpower her with my charm and sophistication. I knew the worst that could happen is that she would say no and I would be emotionally crushed and probably never ask another girl for a date. I would have to enter the priesthood, and I'm not even Catholic.

She said yes. I was completely amazed. I quickly realized that having Lori accept my invitation was the easy part. I now had to confront my parents with the prospect. If there is one thing I had learned in my short life it was, "Timing is everything." Famous last words for sure. My mother didn't really see any problems with the whole issue and agreed, albeit on a somewhat limited basis.

Okay, there may have been a certain amount of whining and pleading on my part, but overall, I'd rate my dancing an even 9.0.

I think my mom's take on things was that Lori was someone she knew and was responsible. Mom was counting on the fact that since Lori was older than me that she wouldn't have any romantic interest in me.

Thus began the first of many experiences. My driving experience was limited to my 1969 four door Pontiac Bonneville that was approximately 87 feet long. It took a quarter tank of gas just to start the thing. All the dents didn't seem to help the allure of the car either. Lori drove a 1969 Camaro convertible, with a manual transmission. I had never driven a manual transmission before. By our third date Lori was teaching me to drive a stick. Older women can teach young guys so much about life.

I may have been a little intimidated by dating an older woman too. Eventually we kissed. We did it a lot, and I guess she must have felt I really needed the practice. There were days I'd go home and my lips would be completely numb and swollen to boot. But hey I was playing it cool as a cucumber, taking it nice and slow so as not to spook Lori with my overwhelming prowess. Either that or I was scared to death. I get confused sometimes.

The Cabin

My best friend, Bob, was a nice responsible kid that my parents seemed to like a lot. He had been dating his girlfriend, Lea, for about a year and things were beginning to get serious. One day Bob and I sat down to compare notes and discuss women at length. The conversation must have lasted all of five minutes. After being married for nearly 20 years I've not learned much more.

Bob and I determined that we must take action, time was of the essence and we weren't getting any younger. We decided that we would spend the weekend at my family's cabin in the mountains, and invite the girls to join us.

We told our parents that we were going up to the lake to do some ice fishing.

It was early June, which in most areas of the world means late spring or early summer. In Montana, this means late winter. In a string of good luck our parents agreed, with some stipulations. We could only stay one night and I had to be home by 11:00 am on Saturday because we were going out of town for a few days.

Lea would be staying at a "friends" house. Lori didn't need permission. We all agreed on a meeting place outside of town on the way to the cabin.

It was a perfect plan. What could possibly go wrong?

On Friday I went to pick up Bob at his house only to learn that Lea couldn't go, some kind of female problem. In all the years since, I have never, for the life of me, been able to figure out what that phrase meant. The only female problem my wife has ever alluded to is her husband. After a brief discussion, I advised Bob that he could no longer go fishing with me.

While driving to the rendezvous point to meet Lori, the muffler fell off of my Bonneville. Initially that didn't seem like much of a problem, it just gave my car a meaner sound. As I was passing through town I stopped by a convenience store to pick up a soda when I noticed flames shooting out from under the hood of my car. Luckily there were two guys in the store, Bill and Ed, who were seniors in high school, who rushed outside with a fire extinguisher. They opened the hood and put out the fire. Since I did not have the air cleaner on the carburetor, they were able to poke the nozzle of the extinguisher right into the carburetor to put out the flames. The down side of this was that my car was now dead. I mean all four legs up. Dead.

I was in a bit of a panic at this point. I had waited my whole life for this one day and it was quickly turning into a disaster. I decided to just forget about the car and find a way to meet Lori and go to the cabin. Like that would have taken a lot of thought.

I approached Bill and Ed and asked for a ride out to the lake. As luck would have it, they were headed out to their cabin on a nearby lake and agreed to drop me off along the way. They were both seniors in high school while I was a lowly junior, so it was quite an honor for them to even acknowledge my existence. Getting lucky at every turn, or so I thought.

On our way out of town Bill drove about 80 in a 35 mph zone. He and Ed decided to smoke and began to roll their own cigarettes. While I initially thought this was enterprising, the sweet smell resembled how people described marijuana. I was vaguely familiar that marijuana slows "everything" down in your system. Just what I didn't want to have happen that night. I was sitting in the back seat and immediately rolled down the window and stuck my head out, while at the same time trying not to appear too conspicuous. This was especially difficult at 11:30 pm on a day in early June, in Montana. The wind chill almost instantaneously caused me to lose all of the feeling in my face. This pretty much took my mind off the fact that I would probably spend mind off the fact that I would probably spend the rest of my life in jail for being an accomplice. After what seemed like hours, we reached the parking lot of an old restaurant and hotel. Lori's car was there and I asked Bill to pull up along side it. I grabbed my sleeping bags and duffel bag, throwing them into Lori's car. Bill and Ed just sat there and watched. I thanked them for the ride and Lori and I were off to the cabin.

As we drove I recounted the events of the evening. As I'd done every moment since reaching puberty I pondered my probability for success. I'd already risked my life at least three or four times already, there was no way anything was going to stop me. Just no way!

When we got near to the lake, about 400 yards from the cabin, Lori's car got stuck in a two-foot snowdrift. I spent an hour trying to dig the car out with no success. It was now 3:00 am. I kept telling myself this night was definitely going to happen no matter what.

I gathered my sleeping bags and suitcase and we commenced the hike through the snow down to the cabin. My first job was to get the furnace started, without success. Next, I pulled the two couches to form a "V" in front of the fireplace to hold in the heat and started a fire. I had brought in a load of firewood in hopes that it would thaw out enough to burn. It wasn't too long before we had a roaring fire.

Suddenly there was a loud pop, like a big firecracker exploded. I looked around the fireplace and could see that it had heated too quickly and there was now a crack running all the way across the top. My dad was going to kill me. The fireplace was new and my dad would know it was me who'd done it. This was the first time all night that I actually felt fear. Yet in spite of it all, I was a man with a mission. Everything else was forgotten in my single-minded 16-year-old determination.

Things were beginning to look brighter.

It was about this time Lori opened a bottle of wine, the kind with a screw top, and poured each of us a glass. I placed my glass on the floor, sat down on the carpet and leaned back against the couch to finally relax. So of course, my glass of wine spills on my mom's light mauve carpet, leaving a purple spot about two feet in diameter. Trying to get a dark wine stain out of a light mauve carpet cannot be done. At least I wasn't able to do it. I actually wondered if anyone would notice the two-foot circular stain in the carpet right in front of the fireplace.

And yet, I was a man on a mission. I unzipped the sleeping bags and laid one atop the other. Lori and I got between the sleeping bags and started to cuddle. As I lay there in her arms, I, well, fell asleep.

When I at last awakened, the room was bright from the reflection of the sun off the snow and through the windows. It seemed early, I was guessing around 7:00 am. We still had plenty of time before I had to get home.

Lori was next to me, staring at me. We began kissing and one thing led to another. Finally, I was within just fractions of an inch from completing my life's goal. Just fractions of an inch.

When suddenly there was a loud booming noise. Someone was outside the cabin, pounding on the door. Then, my mom yelled, "Rick are you in there?"

Oh, my God. I was going to be killed.

I jumped up, dressing wildly as I went. I could see the tag of my turtleneck sweater and knew it was inside out and backwards, I didn't care. I stood at the door, buttoning my jeans. As I swung the door open I looked over at Lori who was still getting dressed, standing there without a shirt or bra. The first thought that ran through my mind was "nice." But then I was jerked back into reality and slammed the door shut. Right in my parents' faces. I was in so much trouble.

My dad yelled, "Open this door right now!"

I was only able to stammer out, "Okay, sorry about that." By now Lori was dressed anyway.

As I opened the door my dad came rushing in, fearing that I might try to slam the door again.

My mom began to yell, "Lori, I can't believe you're that kind of girl."

For a fleeting moment I thought I was going to make it out of this one. I was ready to jump in and voice my agreement if it would have helped keep me alive. My dad grabbed my left arm and was squeezing so tight that his fingernails cut into my skin causing me to bleed. I pulled away from the pain and fell on top of the firewood that I'd brought in the night before. I fell on a piece with a broken branch that pierced my back. Now I was bleeding all over the place.

As my parents yelled, I repeatedly protested our innocence. They were having no part of it though. After they repeated comments in various degrees of loudness, using different voice inflections each time, they sent Lori off to her car and directed my clean-up activity.

When we got up the hill to my parents car, Lori was of course waiting there, her car stuck in the snow. My dad and I pushed it out of the snow bank and we all drove off. Lori was in front of us. I sat in the back seat of my parents orange station wagon with the faux wood paneling along the side.

As we rounded a curve in the roadway that passes by the restaurant where I'd met Lori that previous evening, a car passed us. I didn't pay much attention to it at first. After passing us on the left hand side, it began passing Lori's car. Suddenly it began to slow down again until it was right next to us. It was Bill and Ed. They drove along side us, waving and honking and laughing. My parents didn't know what was going on at this point but their antics only seemed to fuel the fire for round two. The penalty phase.

My parents never did believe that nothing had "happened" between Lori and I. I'll admit that it wasn't for lack of effort. By Monday morning word of my adventure had spread throughout school. I endured taunting and jokes the rest of my days in high school.

I hadn't talked to Bob since high school graduation. We both went our separate ways and led very different lives. It's funny though, after 22 years, I received an email from him. I have no idea how he found me. The first thing he asks is, "Hey, do you remember that girl you got caught at the cabin with?"

The Price of Copper

In 1980, I was a high school senior. My father had worked for The Company for 30 years. At one time it was the fifth largest copper producer in the world.

Our town had a smelting operation that had originally been constructed in the 1800's, and was moved to a new site and rebuilt in the 1920's. While The Company had brought in new smelting technologies as they were developed, the foundation of the smelter facility was a very old plant.

Throughout the 1970's the Environmental Protection Agency (EPA) was intent on ensuring that the emissions the smelter was sending into the atmosphere were within its standards. Each time a helicopter flew overhead everyone in town knew it to be the EPA and that an article would soon appear in the local paper about the emissions.

In chemistry class we learned about chemical emissions. As an experiment, we hung a pair of pantyhose on a laundry line outside. Within weeks we could see them dissolving right before our very eyes. Luckily there was no one wearing them at the time. When the wind was just right, which was almost every day, the pungent smell of sulfur hung over the valley.

For years The Company had been pouring millions of dollars into retrofitting the existing equipment and processes to bring operations up to EPA requirements.

The economic recession that the United States was going through at that time did not bypass the copper industry, The Company, or our sleepy little town. Copper, the main product of the smelting operation, was selling for about $0.82 per pound on the open market and the smelter was producing 24,000 tons of it each month. One might consider it a small drawback but it cost The Company $1.19 per pound to produce. It doesn't take a mathematician to figure out that you can go broke quick by selling a product for 75 percent of what it costs to make. You can't make up the difference in volume either.

During the 1970's the copper industry was really feeling the pinch of foreign competition, especially from Japan and Germany, where higher quality product and lower cost was impacting the U.S. market.

Montana was, without exception, a "Union" state. Nothing was accomplished without a workers' union being involved. The workers at The Company were some of the highest paid people in the United States. There were some laborers who earned $80 dollars per hour. The union made sure that mining employees were well paid for their work.

Unions have been extremely effective at creating a safe haven for its workers over the last century. The level of control that unions have over business has resulted in its members holding an attitude of entitlement - "more money and less work," which seemed to permeate people's work ethic. Keep in mind that an 18-year-old growing up in the midst of it formed this viewpoint. Unfortunately, this kind of attitude is now quite widespread across all stratums of workers in all industries.

The late 1970's were a time when the term "union-busting" was coined. Unions were being asked to give concessions in pay and benefits in an effort to keep entire industries afloat and competitive with foreign rivals.

Strikes are a nasty business of intimidation. Families are forced into poverty-like conditions. Workers more loyal to their family than the union who bravely cross the picket line are known as "Scabs." Strikers shout threats and demeaning expletives at them and sometimes vandalize their cars or even their homes. All too often a person crossing a picket line will be found murdered.

As a small child I remember a strike lasting more than eight months. During the strike my father worked as a mechanic for a friend who owned a modest automobile dealership.

It was a difficult time for our family. Family friends moved away because they couldn't find work and needed to support their family.

Several people were mysteriously killed after crossing the picket line, their murderers never brought to justice. It's safe to say that the amount of money workers lose during a strike can never be regained by any increase in salary they might win. Strikes pit employee against management and create a lose-lose situation. The amount of distrust and contempt between the two groups only serves to strengthen the Union organizers' hold on both.

In 1980, the Union contracts came due for the miners working at the smelter. The word on the street was that a strike was imminent. The Company called a meeting of the managers at their Denver headquarters and told everyone, point blank, that with the price of copper being lower on the market compared to the high cost of production, the plant would be closed down if the union held a strike. They also were told of the domino effect this would force on the entire U.S. operation. In short, new state-of-the-art plants would be built in Japan that would allow The Company to be competitive and profitable in copper production.

With this information in hand, the word was quickly leaked to everyone in town, union and management alike were aware of what was about to happen. The Union voted for a strike, calling The Company's bluff. The Company immediately closed the plant and began demolition even though there were open construction contracts that had to be honored. A new three-story office building, built for the Safety Department my father worked in, was demolished the day construction was completed.

The Company had given the town several million dollars to promote new industry to town. Incompetent politicians and disreputable business people quickly frittered the money away.

In the years since, The Company was acquired by a larger mining concern. The townspeople regularly sue the new parent company for any type of damage imaginable.

Twenty years later the town is a depressing place to visit. No one seems to smile anymore and the townspeople are bitter. Montana ranks almost last in per capita income and near the top in unemployment.

My father was lucky though, through the years he had been able to work his way into management. At the time of the strike he and his peers performed the shutdown and security functions. He was then transferred 1,500 miles to a facility in New Mexico, a uranium mining operation. I was a freshman in college at the time and began spending summers in New Mexico.

The unions, in their greed for control over its members and power over The Company, changed the course of many lives. Personally I hated the Union for what it had done to my life, my family, my town. It took the foundation of my life, the mountains, away from me.

Upon entering the work force I already knew my responsibilities. Philosophically I choose to be personally responsible for ensuring that the business I work for is profitable and competitive, whatever my position on the organizational chart. If my manager makes a bad decision it is because I failed to provide them with the right information or to convince them otherwise. No one said work was easy, and that's why we call it work.

In the modern age of technology, we have instantaneous tools to evaluate how successful we are performing and the profitability of our business. We can compute the quality and cost of producing a product and even compare it to the competition. Unfortunately it is the personalities, power, hidden agendas and unethical personal benefit that drive too many people.

Skiing

High school is an interesting and exciting time for most kids. It promotes the acquisition of knowledge and offers the challenge to perform higher level thought processes about mathematics, science, English, art, music, and history. My grades during high school were not what you'd call consistent. A lot had to do with the quality of the teacher and their level of compassion and sympathy. The subjects that I liked best never seemed to like me all that much. Let's put it this way, if my grades during high school were put in a pot of soup you'd be able to spell quite a few words.

It was during high school that I was stricken with a disease that impacted my ability to speak and focus thoughts beyond any girl standing even remotely in my vicinity. Whenever I attempted to speak my voice would fluctuate, hitting all octaves at once. The mere thought of a girl, with her soft looking hair and smelly teen perfume was enough to send my heart rate skyrocketing. It was during this time that I first noticed my eye-hand coordination was beginning to deteriorate. This was particularly troublesome since it wasn't all that good to begin with. I walked into the edge of our bathroom door so many times that I feared there would be a permanent two-inch stripe running down my forehead.

The pursuit of knowledge was a goal way too lofty for my intellect so I spent my high school days chasing girls and trying to play sports. During my day, girls didn't like brainy guys, so I played sports to try and impress them.

Unfortunately, the girls I knew didn't much care for me which was a shame since I was far from being brainy.

My later high school years were marred by a series of unfortunate accidents that were truly unique. During football, coach always made a point of telling me to keep my head down. The first time I took the advice was on a kick-off when I was running flat out down the field and collided with a guy that resembled a goal post. When I woke up I discovered my sternum was broken from the impact of my helmet's facemask against my chest.

In late winter of my junior year I was involved in what would have been a dramatic ski accident if it weren't so comical. A friend and I were skiing along a giant slalom run at one of the local ski areas. The temperature was –24 degrees and was so cold that our eyelashes froze together. That wouldn't have been so bad, I suppose, if we hadn't been skiing straight down along the tree line of the expert runs. My heart rate certainly got a big boost at the point I lost my eyesight. I immediately begin prying my eyelids apart and rubbing them with the palm of my hands. I had pried one eye open as I glided onto a jump, consisting of some stacked hay bails covered in ice. By the time I reached the end of the jump, a matter of milliseconds at my current rate of travel, I had somehow caught the edge of a ski in an ice rut. This had the affect of propelling me into the air with such force that my body cartwheeled out of control. I was still trying to open my eyes although I was better off not knowing what was happening. As my body began to touch down, the friction caused me to lose anything not permanently affixed to me. First my skis came whizzing off, then my hat, gloves, a boot, and my jacket. I felt like Charlie Brown after Lucy pulled the football away as I lay face down in the snow. Somehow, when one of my skis came off, it was propelled straight into the outer atmosphere. Upon reentry it must have activated a homing device because it came right to me. Actually it came right at me, hitting me squarely in the back.

Since I was only wounded but still alive and all appendages mostly operable, my parents ruled me fit for duty and kept me going to school.

It was the middle of wrestling season and my win-loss record began to reflect that something might be wrong. Not knowing any better, I exercised more often thinking I needed to improve my physical condition.

By early summer going into my senior year, my mom commissioned me to excavate the dirt and rock from under our house to expand the half-basement into a full basement. In exchange, she bought me my first car, a Pontiac Bonneville, for $125 dollars.

At the same time, my granduncle hired me to put down gravel and grade the driveway leading to the cabin. It seems that cars were getting stuck too often. While I can attest to that fact, I didn't offer my opinion or particular experience with cars getting stuck at the cabin. It was information that only would have served to queer the deal. My wages were a nice and tidy $2 per hour.

Being a crafty entrepreneur, I loaded our pick-up truck with the rock and dirt from our basement and hauled it to the cabin for disposal. Essentially being paid for each end of the trip.

Being more heavily armed with brawn than brains, indeed a scary thought, I did my best to carry the granite boulders up the basement stairs and load them into the truck. I'm guessing that's probably why that particular area of Montana is called "The Rocky Mountains." It was, literally, back breaking work, as I soon found out. For some reason my parents refused to provide me with the proper tools, such as dynamite, to be effective in my work.

Midway through the summer as I was almost finished excavating the basement, and with the driveway complete, the toil caught up with my back. Even though I hadn't quite met the prerequisites for a doctor appointment, my parents begrudgingly took me to be examined when I started to lose feeling in my legs.

I spent the remaining half of summer either in traction at the hospital or in traction at home. What a perfect way for an active young boy to spend the summer.

Throughout my senior year I only attended about three or four months of school. The rest of the time I traveled around the state having medical tests and surgeries of varying intensity of pain. I spent the time during the winter Olympic games having surgery to fuse two vertebrate together. Even though the doctor told me I'd have a 70 percent chance of being paralyzed from the waist down and have to undergo at least three more major surgeries, I spent the time plotting my comeback to ski the giant slalom and downhill events at the next Olympic games.

When I finally returned to school it turned out that I earned the best grades of my entire high school career. If I'd have known about that potential, years earlier, I could have saved both the teachers and me a whole lot of aggravation. If I would have played my cards right I probably could have made straight "A's" just by missing a few more classes.

Boxing

On one of my numerous hospital internments resulting from my ski accident I was released the day before my birthday. To celebrate, my friend Mark and I traveled to Butte to cruise Harrison Avenue, also known as "the drag" on Friday and Saturday nights. There were a bunch of girls our age standing in the parking lot of a local fast food restaurant so we parked around the corner to avoid anyone seeing our license plate and recognizing we were from Anaconda, their archrivals. As we stood there talking the local guys showed up. Eventually someone recognized us as being from Anaconda and we were quickly surrounded. Then the pushing and shoving started. Mark and I made a break for his car with about 50 people trailing behind us. As he fumbled for his car keys a group of about 20 guys approached and started hitting us from behind. I took off running down the street hoping that they would follow me and allow Mark to open the car door. Most of them did come after me and after a ways I turned and ran directly through the crowd, wildly swinging my fists at every face I could see. When I got back to the car, four guys had Mark down on the ground and were kicking him. I knocked them out of the way and Mark got up and got into his car. Before I could open my door, they knocked me down and started kicking me. I grabbed someone's leg as his boot struck my face and pulled him to the ground. We were lying in the gutter and I started hitting him as hard as I could in the face. Blood started coming from his ear. I got to my knees and swung at another guy, hitting him just about waist high. He screeched and fell in such a way that I was able to make my break and get into the car. About five carloads of guys chased us for several miles out of town. So much for a bitter rivalry.

My previous experience with fighting came from my older brother who would regularly teach me the fine of art of getting beaten to a pulp. I guess all the frustration from years of being on the receiving end was unleashed just in the nick of time.

After graduation I attended a small Catholic college in Montana's capital city of Helena. My mother and grandmother had graduated from the same college and my father spent a great deal of time there too, pursuing my mother. My mother thought it would teach me some good study habits. I thought that with all the guys going to school to become priests I would be in demand with the ladies.

The day before classes began, there was an ice cream social to introduce the students to one another. Since it was a hot August day, some enterprising young lads substituted kegs of beer for the ice cream. It was a big disappointment to almost everyone in attendance. The first group of people I met was from Butte and we instantly became good friends, probably because we had so much in common – namely all the acrimony we held for each other.

Since not attending classes had done so well for me during my senior year in high school, I figured it was worth the effort to give it a try at college. Given the amount of free time this provided me, I chose to pursue extracurricular opportunities. Since all the extracurricular opportunities I was interested in refused to have anything to do with me, I again tried sports.

About mid-way through the fall semester I saw a poster in the dormitory's mailroom advertising tryouts for the boxing team. I began a regimented training program for the first time in my life, getting up before class each morning to run three miles and then working out after classes. A man, reportedly from the FBI, showed up at practice one day. He told us that since we were trained fighters if we got into a brawl out in public it would be our fault, no matter who started it. The only thing that went through my mind was – oh sure, somebody picks a fight with me, beats me up, and I get all the blame. Sounded just like being at home with my sisters.

I was a welterweight boxer, which is in the middle of the weight classes. This means that the lighter boxers were much quicker than I and the heavier boxers carried a bigger punch. When it came time to spar it was always such a difficult decision. Do I repeatedly get punched by the little guys or get hit really hard by the big guys? Decisions, decisions. One of the heavyweight boxers resembled my older brother so I felt compelled to let him pound on me. On one occasion he beat me so badly that the entire left side of my face was bruised, including my hair. Bruised hair really hurts, bad.

Once we ceased being a complete and total embarrassment to our coaches, exhibition matches were scheduled to allow us to gain experience boxing in front of a crowd. Our first fight was at a bar that looked to be frequented by old-time loggers who had spent their youth in mental hospitals. At least one of them still had all his teeth.

The tables had been cleared out in the middle of the bar and a ring set up. Inside the ring I was a little claustrophobic since the ceiling, comprised of rough-sawn wood held up by log beams, was mere inches from the top of my head. I was just glad that I was one of the shorter boxers. After our bouts, the barkeep treated us to nice thick gristly steak and those big fat french fries that were soaked with grease. At least the food was good.

The big event was the Junior Class Smoker, held in the Helena sports arena. There was a crowd of over 3,000 people, which was pretty good since there were only 1,000 students attending the college. All the politicians showed up, probably because all the local media was present.

Each bout was scheduled for three rounds, with two minutes in each round. The roar of the crowd was frightening and I was scared to death. Fighting in a bar in front of drunken loggers is one thing, but the potential for being completely pummeled in front of the entire college, state government, and captured by the media for posterity, was just a little overwhelming.

Getting dressed in the locker room took all of my remaining energy and I could barely hold my hands up for the coach to wrap them in tape. My name was called over the loud speaker. My heart was pounding so hard I thought it was trying to escape.

The walk to the ring seemed to take hours. It took all the strength of the two female escorts to force me out of the locker room and push me up the steps to the ring. I would have been able to hold onto the locker room door jam longer if I hadn't been wearing boxing gloves. If only the escorts weren't holding me up by my ankles and pulling me toward the ring.

Once the bell rang, my opponent, Kevin, and I met in the middle of the ring. I tried to engage him in conversation to ease his anxiety and perhaps prolong my life. He seemed intent on hitting me though. I tried my best imitation of Mohammed Ali's fancy footwork but my shoes seemed to be glued to the floor. It's a little known fact but the gravity inside a boxing ring is five times greater than normal earth gravity. This makes a ten-ounce boxing glove outside the ring weigh something like three pounds inside the ring. The number of people watching the bout causes the inside-the-ring weight to be multiplied. So in this case I figure my boxing gloves weighed something like 120 pounds each.

As we stood toe-to-toe in the center of the ring, swinging wildly at one another, I was afraid that one of us might actually hit the other. At some point during the match one of us started bleeding enough so that both of us were covered in tiny red polka dots. My opponent and I punched, parried, blocked, ducked, danced and dodged. Without a doubt this was the longest six minutes of my life, not counting my wedding vows. Although, after all these years it doesn't really matter who won the fight though, we both fought valiantly.

The one trophy I ever won, a brass figure of a boxer, now sits atop a bookcase in my eight-year-old son's bedroom. It is all tarnished with age and is wedged in between his karate, basketball and academic trophies. The little show-off, always having to rub it in.

A photograph, an action shot, of Kevin and I boxing made it to the front page of the newspaper and in the college yearbook. Both places managed to get my name wrong though.

My academics didn't progress as well as I had anticipated. It seems that there's some kind of correlation between attending classes, doing homework, taking tests and making good grades. Although I continued my experimentation to achieve good grades by doing as little homework and class attendance as possible, it never really achieved the level of success I had hoped. It took me over ten years to payoff the tuition loan but it was well worth it.

Marriage

Marriage is the ultimate adventure that many attempt but few survive. A recent news report stated that one out of two marriages end in divorce. Surviving a climb of Mt. Everest has better odds. Another study says that men are first concerned with a woman's looks while women are primary concerned with a man's wealth, an arrangement that I thought was illegal in all states except Nevada. It sounds like the world's oldest profession has made its way into mainstream society. So much for the equal rights movement.

I've always heard that the main reason husbands and wives fight is over money. All these studies make me wonder if the main cause of divorce is because the husband doesn't earn enough or the wife got ugly.

There is a saying, "When the going gets tough the tough get going." Apparently they are going straight to divorce court.

Not only do people seem eager to get a divorce, many also like to watch the misery unfold. Courtroom drama and salacious details of infidelity are shown right on daytime television.

If I recall correctly a part of the standard marriage vows includes, among others, a promise to stay married until "death do us part."

Perhaps the lawyers won a class action suit against God and government to get a reprieve on the marriage vows as a non-binding contract. Perhaps folks just crossed their fingers behind their backs, making it okay not to fulfill the promise. To end a marriage in divorce is to say their promises were frivolous. To break a promise that has such huge consequences means that there is no promise worthy of being kept.

Not only have divorce rates exponentially increased but bankruptcy rates also have skyrocketed. Bankruptcy is a legal way to steal from other people. Once upon a time it was a huge stigmatism and people were ostracized within their communities for declaring bankruptcy. Now it's all the rage. It would seem that anyone willing to steal from another and then blatantly wag their tongue at the victim certainly has a lot of brevity, if nothing else.

During the 1980's, we saw the "me" generation, signified by yuppies and their conspicuous consumption. During the 1990's, we saw the "your" generation as in "my problems are all your fault."

I wonder what some parents, too many parents, must be telling their children. Oh they might not be saying the words, but, even worse, setting the example.

"Suzy, where did you get that bicycle?"

"Gee Mom, I took it from our neighbor's garage."

"Did anyone see you take it?"

"No, Mom."

"Okay dear, in that case you can go ahead and keep it."

"Hey Dad, can I go outside and play?"

"Johnny, you promised to do your homework before going outside. Did you get it completed?"

"No Dad, I don't really feel like it."

"Okay son, have a good time with your friends."

"Hi Mom, I'm home from school."

"Johnny, did you get your report card today?"

"Yes mom, I got C's and D's."

"Oh my dear Lord, how come you got D's?"

"The teachers don't like me."

"Oh that school hires the worst teachers, I'm going down there and tell them off."

Throughout my son's grade school there are posters that remind students to wait their turn in line, to be courteous and to follow through on their commitments. It's too bad that so many adults didn't learn these basic concepts.

After my sophomore year of college I traveled from Montana to stay with my parents over the summer at their home in New Mexico. After getting a job as a cook at a local truck stop I enrolled in summer classes at the local college, a branch of New Mexico State University.

On the first day of class I met my wife, although neither of us knew it at the time. It was a public speaking course held in a tiny wedge-shaped classroom. There were about ten people in the class. I had been sitting in the back row, leaning my chair back so it rested against the wall. A petite girl with black hair walked into class as the bell rang. She was dressed in rust colored slacks and matching blouse. I watched as she walked along the back wall.

She paused as she approached where I was sitting and looked down at me, "Excuse me, may I get past?"

She shook her head from side-to-side as she walked past me and I knew it was probably because she needed to clear her mind of the impression I made.

With each class she would sit farther and farther from me. Being a man of the world I knew she was playing hard to get. I followed her out to the parking lot one day and asked for a date. Unfortunately, she had to get her car washed, although it already looked sparkling clean to me. Eventually, as the weeks went by, and after she'd cleaned and repaired just about everything her family owned, Carrie agreed to meet me for lunch.

Since it was a special date, I decided to splurge. Being a poor college kid, splurging meant going to McDonalds. She had a Big Mac and I had a Fillet O' Fish sandwich. I later learned that she hated eating at McDonalds.

After several weeks, Carrie broke up with me because her dad didn't like me and forbade her to see me. Apparently he thought I was just a hick from Montana and just not good enough for his daughter. Carrie and her dad seemed to think a lot alike. We stayed apart for almost an entire week before sneaking to see each other. We'd plan to meet at the college, my work or her brother's house. Our dates, primarily due to my financial situation, consisted of hiking and picnics on the mountain, an inactive volcano, looming behind the town.

The mountains are a great place to have a date during the daytime. Although a relationship can be jeopardized by nightfall when strange creatures start lurking about making all sorts of crackling, creaking, croaking, cooing and popping noises. Romance is in the air, hearts are racing, then a strange noise echoes nearby in the night and in an instant you are trying to outrace your date to the car hoping that whatever is out there will get her before it gets you.

The problem with living in a town of less than 10,000 people is that everyone knows your business. After a few months of dating, Carrie's mom found out. Eventually she agreed to our dating and even began working on Carrie's dad to acquiesce.

The first few times I went over to Carrie's house for dinner I was more than a little uncomfortable to say the least. It was difficult being around people that didn't like me all that much, although with my family I should have been use to it. Ultimately, I wore down Carrie's defenses and despite her feelings for me we married just over a year later.

During the first year of our marriage we moved to Albuquerque where I attended college full-time and held a full-time job working at an electrical parts company. Even though we both worked, there was little money left over after payday. After paying our bills we usually had $20 dollars remaining for the next two weeks to spend on whatever we wanted. Usually we'd go have dinner and catch a movie – a cheap hamburger and a discount movie theater.

During our second year of marriage I was injured in a work related accident and spent over a year in the hospital or confined to bed. Because insurance covered 25 percent of my salary, we lived off of Carrie's salary. To say that times were tough is an understatement. Oddly enough, whenever Carrie's parents came to visit they would end up going grocery shopping and bought too many groceries. Her mom would say she was still in the habit of cooking for a large family and they would end up dumping a bunch of food on us. Not wanting to hurt their feelings we graciously accepted the extra food. As a matter of fact, we still have a box of cherry cake mix in the pantry that has followed us as we've moved around the country.

As a result of my accident, the doctors told me that I could no longer do any type of manual labor and needed to get a desk job. It was the mid-1980's and banks were in crisis due to corruption and inefficiency. In all my arrogance I decided that I could fix these problems and got a job as a part-time teller, earning $300 dollars a month.

Slowly, but monotonously, we began improving our station in life.

Neither Carrie nor I was permitted to cause an automobile accident because we were lucky to have insurance, on the rare occasions when we had insurance that is. In my life, the only automobile accidents I had ever been in were during the first several years of our marriage. Late November each year I would be stopped at a red light and someone would hit me from behind. It was always just hard enough to cause a couple hundred dollars worth of damage, mostly just bending the bumper and scraping the paint. I would get parts from a junkyard and do the repairs myself. I used the left over money to buy Carrie's Christmas presents.

After several years of being married our combined annual income exceeded $20,000. We were finally wealthy.

I worked hard at my job and ended up being promoted several times. Because of the bank's compensation policies, my salary trailed far behind my responsibilities. It was about this time that I learned about as much as I could and arrogantly decided to sell my services to a bank that would be willing to pay for the experience. I quit my job and drove out to California. I had never been to California before so this was an exciting trip. I had to travel at night because my car regularly overheated in the desert sun.

For a few days I stayed with a sister who lived in Los Angeles. Whenever she would introduce me to someone it was always, "This is my brother Rick, we're supporting him while he looks for work." My sister. I have to love her because any other emotion would end up causing me time in jail.

After California we moved to Arizona then on to Iowa, Michigan and Texas. Each stay lasted between two and five years, not too unlike a prison sentence for at least one of those moves. With each move Carrie would stay behind and get the house ready to be rented or sold and organize the moving while working full-time. It would usually be three months before she would join me, mainly because we both wanted to make sure my new job was going to work out. Once our child, Christian, was born Carrie would become a single parent during the transition, seeing me only a few times each month. My job was to find a new house and get it into move-in condition.

During our marriage there have easily been thousands of events and arguments that could have undermined it. I was to blame for at least one of them. To say we had hard times would truly be an understatement. Carrie and I know each other's hot buttons and we've been known to push them all at the same time. But, the basic premise of our marriage is a promise to one another. Because we both stand behind our promises, divorce could never be an option to solve a problem, no matter how big that problem could be. No matter how bad things got we always know we have to somehow resolve the conflict.

Marriage isn't about compromise, it's about being considerate, caring, loving, and compassionate. Life is a series of choices. Each day we make decisions about which things matter and which don't. Marriage is a lot of hard work.

In recent years I've heard that athletes have morality clauses in their contracts. It's as if people can't remember, all by their lonesome, to behave themselves. Perhaps all marriages should have formal written contracts and spell out the specific terms. The husband must maintain a certain net worth. The attractiveness of the wife may never vary from certain wedding-day specifications. Anniversaries would be marked by a contract review between the lawyers to see if either party had violated the terms of the agreement. There could be renewable terms of the agreement, say every six months. That way people wouldn't get divorced, their contract would just simply expire and both people would then be free to negotiate with other parties. Providing that the Vice Squad doesn't monitor negotiations.

I guess every wedding would have a lawyer as the best man and maid of honor. The preacher also would be a judge. The ceremony could take place in a courtroom and the wedding guests, now called witnesses, would be called upon to testify on the financial records of the groom and the attractiveness of the bride. The job of the ring bearer would be to make sure fingers aren't crossed.

Cycling In Snake Country

As a boy, my only mode of transportation other than my feet was my bicycle. Even though it was a single speed model, having it opened up a whole new world to me. My mother and father would have laughed if I even hinted at their driving me to a friend's house.

It all started one sunny, spring morning when my father built my first bike out of the many surplus parts created as my older brother and sister wore out their bikes.

My bike was a hybrid, having parts from nearly all vintages of bicycles. Dad carefully measured me and then permanently welded the adjustable parts, which didn't quite fit together, such as the seat and handle bars. Having them permanently fixed meant that within a few weeks I had outgrown the bike. But I was forced to continue riding it for the next few years.

While all my friends had fancy banana bikes, where the seat was shaped like a large banana, mine had a seat that looked like a hatchet head, just not as comfortable. My bike, the same color as our garage, didn't have a chain guard so the bottom inside of every right pant leg was missing a large chunk and stained dark brown from oil.

Every day I would test the boundaries set by my parents, traveling further and further from home. My friends and I roamed the game trails in the wilderness area behind our row of houses. Having a bicycle gave us a certain level of confidence that if we ran into a wild animal we could escape.

Since I depended on my bicycle so much, I worked on it regularly. Even though it worked fine, I felt the need to fix it. At first I would just tip it upside down so that it rested on the seat and handlebars. I hand cranked the pedals to apply oil. The bike chain needed lots of oil because it kept getting wiped off by pant leg.

On one very painful occasion, my finger got caught between the chain and the sprocket. A single speed bike only pedals in one direction because the backward pedaling motion sets the brake. Therefore, to get my finger out, I had to force the pedals forward. The end of my index finger now has a permanent half twist.

After that experience I chose to focus my repair efforts on other parts of the bike.

My bike didn't have a kickstand so I had to either prop it up against something, like a fence or wall, or lay it on the ground. One day I traveled to my friend, Chris's house. He and some other friends were playing in his front yard. I leaned my bike against the rear bumper of his dad's truck and went off to play. A few hours later, when it was time for me to go home, I found my bike leaning against their fence. At first it didn't look like my bike because it was all bent and twisted. It was obvious what had happened though. Chris's dad failed to check behind his truck before backing out of his driveway and crushed my bike.

I was devastated.

Several months later, as my Christmas present, I received a brand new bike. It was the most beautiful thing I'd ever seen, a candy-apple red banana bike. Santa Claus proved he is the nicest guy in the whole wide world.

One of the many purposes served by my bike was to act as protection against the dogs that lived on our street. They loved to chase cars and children on bicycles. When approaching a house where a big dog would be lurking I would pedal my hardest and build as much speed as I could. Upon seeing me, the dog would come running and I would have to hop off my bike and use it as a shield as I walked. With any luck the dog would give up once I passed out of its territory and into that belonging to the next big dog.

My bicycle served as a horse when we played cowboys and Indians. As a trusty steed it could do any manner of tricks, such as rearing up on its hind legs. It even took many a bullet from rascally outlaws, intended for me.

As we grew, so did the physical abilities of our bikes. When Evil Knieval was jumping his motorcycle over rows of cars and buses, our bicycles where transformed into high-powered and throaty hogs. We built ramps out of bricks and boards to jump anything and everything we could find. We even jumped over younger brothers and sisters until the time Chris missed the ramp and drove over their ankles.

Eventually my interests changed though. A bicycle is great for everything but going on dates. As soon as I acquired a driver license and bought a car I sold my bike in a garage sale to get gas money.

A few years after I married, my wife suggested that we should each get a bicycle and begin exercising. A co-worker who was an avid cyclist engaged me in a conversation about an upcoming race, The Tour Of The Rio Grande Valley. Within a few weeks I spent our life savings on a lightweight-racing model that would have been at home on the Tour De France. It had clipless pedals, like ski bindings, and a computer that was more advanced than anything we owned. To look the part I outfitted myself with the latest in spandex apparel.

Spandex not only has the ability to highlight every bulge, it creates new and even more unsightly bulges by squeezing all the wrong places.

A day before the race I rode my bike for the first time, logging an easy five miles. There were two racecourses, a 50 and 100-mile ride. I chose the 50-mile course. The first half of the course was on a steady downward grade and the return route was filled with hills. By the time I reached the 25-mile marker, my thighs were burning and my feet on fire. I struggled on the return, being passed by young children on their single speed bikes and old people on their three wheel carts.

I resorted to walking up the last few hills, resting frequently on the descent. For the last five miles, my legs were so stiff that I had to walk.

I worked my way up to riding my bicycle 40 miles a day for several months. I rode from our house in a far northwest suburb to Interstate 40 and back again.

My turn around point was a subdivision where the streets had all been surfaced but no homes had yet been built.

One day, as I reached my normal turn around point, I was traveling at a pretty good speed but not paying too much attention and drove my bicycle right next to a snake that was coiled up in the middle of the roadway. Throughout my entire life I have been deathly afraid of snakes, no matter what kind of snake. My immediate reaction was to jerk both feet up to prevent getting bitten. Jerking up both feet while they are affixed to the pedals is not a bright idea. I lost control of the bike and crashed to the ground a few feet away from the snake. With my feet still firmly hooked to the pedals, and gallons of adrenaline coursing through my veins, I used my arms to pull myself away from the snake, dragging the bicycle along behind.

After moving about 25 feet I quickly glanced back to check how closely the snake was pursuing me. To my utter amazement the snake hadn't moved. I unhooked myself from the bicycle and the snake still hadn't moved. Curiosity got the best of me and I reached for a board laying on the ground and proceeded over to the snake to prod it. Surprisingly it was either in shock over watching me trying to get away or it was dead.

My only previous experience with snakes was with prairie rattlers in central Montana. Whenever we'd visit my grandparents ranch we had to be careful playing in the fields because they'd take over gopher holes, which are a bed-n-breakfast for rattlers.

A few weeks later, on a Sunday, as the sun was beginning to set, I took off for a quick 20-mile ride. About half an hour into the ride I was coasting downhill on the outskirts of a residential neighborhood. A small white car coming up the hill turned across the lane right in front of me. I slammed on both brakes but my speed was too great. As I was about to hit the car I threw my bike sideways and broadsided the car. My thigh took the brunt of the impact and crushed the passenger door and my helmet, with my head inside, whipped against the upper door jam, knocking me unconscious. I awoke to the sound of an ambulance and fire trucks approaching. The firemen practiced inserting the IV needle into my arm, which took quite a bit longer than the ride to the hospital, a few blocks away.

After a few weeks of recovery and physical therapy, I sold the bike in our first garage sale. No one wanted the spandex though.

Several years later I took my family on a trip to Montana to visit my grandmother. Afterwards we drove through Yellowstone Park to Jacksonhole, Wyoming. We brought along our bikes so we could take full advantage of the scenery and get some exercise after being cramped inside the car for hours at a time. We stopped at a rest area near the base of the Grand Tetons. The sun was just coming up and cast a golden glow on the mountain peaks. The only sounds were chirps from the birds and gophers.

I unloaded my bike and rode out into a sweeping meadow to snap a few photographs from a different vantage than the horde of tourists coming into the parking lot.

As I stood there taking photos I felt an itch on my left calf muscle, and thought I must have brushed against the thorns of a sticker bush. Without thinking I balanced on my left foot and brushed the laces of my right shoe to scratch the spot.

I packed away my camera and as I started to pedal away noticed blood on my nice white sneakers. I looked at my calf where there were two little holes a half-inch apart, dripping blood. Seeing the bite mark on my leg caused it to throb painfully and I was overcome with a headache and nausea. While it was probably too soon for the venom to affect me, I read somewhere that the first symptoms of a poisonous snakebite are a headache and nausea, so I wanted to make sure I was prepared.

As I pedaled back to the car I could see hundreds of gopher holes all around where I was standing. By the time we reached town my calf had a large black spot five inches in diameter and was swollen to twice its normal size.

Within a few days I was feeling much better.

My bike now hangs in the garage. I'm thinking we need to have another garage sale.

Besides, we still have some spandex clothes we need to get rid of.

POLO

For a time, my wife Carrie and I lived in Canoga Park, a suburb northwest of Los Angeles. Having never lived in such a large and diverse city before, we explored the city on weekends. Our favorite places included the Natural Museum of History and Marina Del Ray where we would park our car along the inlet and watch yachts sailing in and out of the harbor. Our favorite drive was along the Pacific Coast Highway (PCH) through Malibu, something we did each Sunday since moving to California from New Mexico. One day as we were driving along we happened to pass a sign posted in a large field. It advertised "Equestrian Property" which we assumed had to be really expensive horse property. Within a short distance Carrie noticed another sign that advertised equestrian riding lessons and announced that she always thought it would be interesting to play polo because it seems to be such a challenging sport. I had no idea where that thought had come from and just gave her an odd look. As far as I knew Carrie had ridden horses only a few times in her entire life.

Little did I know how such a simple, out-of-the-blue statement could make such a drastic impact on my life.

It always starts out that way in our little family. My wife feigns interest in some dangerous activity, hobby, or sport, and I end up becoming totally obsessed by it. Becoming obsessed with what you are doing is probably the single biggest downside of having an obsessive personality.

When Carrie first mentioned the idea of playing polo, I dismissed it altogether. After all, polo is a sport of the rich and famous. A little too frou-frou for my taste. The few times I had ever seen polo being played was on television. Even then there were only short excerpts showing royalty or rich people riding a horse up and down a field, dressed very stylishly, while the rider

59

hits a little white ball with a long stick. It seemed to me that the horse does all the work.

About two weeks after Carrie made her pronouncement about polo, we traveled to Solvang, a small Danish community (referring to the people not the pastry). While walking through the lobby of the hotel, Carrie spotted a pamphlet among the hundreds of pamphlets displayed along the wall by the hotel's entrance. There, emblazoned on the cover, was a photograph of polo players. For the life of me I can't figure out how she ever saw it. There were hundreds of pamphlets advertising the local attractions and they all shared very similar color schemes. I pulled it out of the rack and looked over the pictures. This particular pamphlet advertised Sunday Polo Matches at a small community outside Santa Barbara that overlooked the Pacific Ocean. Since we would be passing through Santa Barbara on our return home, Carrie wanted to stop and watch a game. Since we were still young and in love I acquiesced to her demand. I hoped it wouldn't be as painful as the time Carrie dragged me to a baseball game, an experience akin to watching paint dry.

We left Solvang early that Sunday morning in order to catch the first of the two polo matches. When we arrived I was rather unimpressed with the turnout and was sure we were in for a very boring day under an oppressive sun. We parked in a grass field opposite the polo fields that offered a short walk to the grandstand seating lining the field.

Carrie purchased a program that described some of the details about the game itself. A polo field is ten acres, the area of nine football fields and measures 300 yards long by 160 yards wide. There are four players on each team. Each player has a rating of –2 to +10 and the sum of the ratings for each team needs to be the same. There are six periods called chukars that last seven minutes each and a 30-second overtime period. I figured that 42 minutes per game would be almost bearable.

A fresh horse is used for each chukar. The number of horses and their tack, along with their room and board and travel expenses, would be why this is a sport of the rich. While the objective of the game is to hit the ball between two upraised goal posts at either end of the field, it was an abject lesson in geometry. Unfortunately for me, I never did get the hang of geometry in school.

The first match teamed up novice players against one another and was fairly similar to the stuff shown on television except that it seemed to last forever. It turns out that Polo is a lot like football in that the time clock is stopped whenever there is a penalty. There were a lot of penalties.

Unlike most spectator sports we could hear how well versed the players were in the use of expletives. They could string cuss words into whole sentences with nary a conjunction. Their attention span, however, must have been quite short because they kept repeating these colorful and well-practiced phrases as if they were afraid of forgetting them.

When I was a kid and my mother would tell me to be home at a certain time, I would repeat that time over and over so as not to forget it. Sure enough though, as soon as I stopped saying it, I would forget it. Although, I did manage to show up at our house fairly frequently and pretty often too.

The second match of the day was much different. Along with the wealthy American benefactor, each team was comprised of professionals hailing from Argentina. There were eight goal players and two ten-goalers. There are very few Polo players in the world to ever achieve a ten-goal rating.

Watching these guys play was nothing short of amazing. It was a fast paced game. The riders held the horse's reigns in one hand and the mallet in the other. Their bottoms were never in the saddle and it appeared that they only stayed on due to the centrifugal force of the speeding horse. The horses would start, stop, and run at great speeds while the riders swung at the ball or blocked an opponent from swinging. The opposing players pushed their horses against one another while running down the field to prevent the other from hitting the ball or getting a good shot.

They hit the ball around the field like it was in a pinball machine. At one point two riders and their horses running about 25 miles an hour approached the ball at right angles to one another and collided. One horse fell on impact and was lying on its rider's leg. The other horse awkwardly stepped on the fallen horse and rider for a brief few seconds. All the players and umpires jumped from their mounts and rushed over to help. The fans sat in the grandstands in complete silence. An ambulance and a truck pulling a horse trailer drove onto the field and entered the fracas. Surprisingly, in an orderly manner the fallen rider, who closely resembled a Picasso painting, was scooped up and put into the ambulance and rushed to the hospital. The horse was carefully evaluated while it lay on the ground with someone draped across its neck to keep it from moving. When the horse got up everyone in the grandstands cheered with relief.

But, our joy was a little too quick. The horse, walking on only three legs, was loaded into the trailer and driven to the far end of the polo grounds. I continued to watch the trailer from our vantage point to see what additional care it would be given. About 15 minutes later I heard a heavy bang and almost instantaneously a loud thud.

The game resumed when a new rider was conscripted and horse readied. The match finished without any further incident.

Completely amazed at the skill of the riders, the aggressiveness of the horses and the level of danger, I was hooked.

Once back in Los Angeles, we searched for more Polo matches. The L.A. Equestrian Center in Burbank, sight of equestrian venues for the 1984 Olympic games, held professional polo matches on Saturday nights. Amateur matches were held at Will Rogers State Park on Sunday afternoon. Of course, there were both professional and amateur matches held in Santa Barbara on Sundays. We began attending a few matches at first, but like a powerfully addictive drug, our attendance quickly accelerated. For my birthday Carrie got me an introductory package of five lessons for $125 dollars. That was about the same amount as a cheap pair of boots or riding pants that I most certainly needed if I was going to look the part. Even buying used stuff was expensive, although at the time my main concern was that someone hadn't been killed using that particular piece of equipment.

The director of the polo school, Vince, was good player in his own right and the father of Mike, a ten-goal player. My instructor, Kendrick, was long-haired and Hollywood handsome. He was polo player in the movie "Pretty Woman."

For the first time in our married life we began budgeting our money. Essentially, my wife's paycheck was spent supporting my addiction. For the next two years I played Polo between three and five times a week and we attended matches every Saturday and Sunday. Carrie's job was to photographically document my progress because I wanted proof that I played polo when I was old and decrepit -which would come sooner than even I anticipated. Although Carrie admits that most of the time, instead of taking photographs, she was cringing in anticipation of me becoming smashed, mashed or squashed.

Kendrick's teaching method was somewhat unique, although it was clear he took a great personal interest in training me and wanted to make sure that I retained the knowledge. Quite often he would practice his use of rare and obsequious expletives that were aimed at my abilities, personage, ancestry, race, religion, sex, you get the idea. Listening to Kendrick's tirades, Carrie always became somewhat agitated. I think sometimes she got mad at him for not using strong enough language. When he took to throwing horse chips at me she really came unglued. I tried to explain to her that I was paying this guy a lot of her money to make me learn and I wasn't concerned with his methods as long as I learned. Her take on it was somewhat different than mine.

Within no time at all I had a vanity license plate on my sport utility vehicle proudly proclaiming my addiction: "POLO." By the end of my second year I had earned the nickname "Gaucho" which is a cowboy in Argentina. However, even though Carrie speaks Spanish fluently, her pronunciation always sounded like she was calling me "Groucho."

From a practical standpoint polo is a sport formed in Persia that is over 700-years-old. Its roots in combat where the horse and rider were trained to meet combatants on the battlefield. The rider was required to guide and protect the horse for which his life depended and at the same time wield a deadly sword to kill his opponents. All without injuring himself or the horse. It wasn't a trivial sport but rather offensive and defensive training for warfare. I'm not quite sure how this relates to my profession as a banker but at some point I must have had a darn good justification.

Real tragedy struck my life when the L.A. Equestrian Center was hit with a double whammy. Brought on by the real estate crunch that hit southern California and a failed Savings and Loan that held the mortgage, the L.A. Equestrian Center was closed pending its sale.

Life was never the same after that.

Within a few months I took a job in Arizona where my research indicated the prospects seemed better for playing polo. My research was looking at the club listings in the polo magazines. They say timing is everything. Mine was awful. Arizona also was being hit by a real estate crisis and a Savings and Loan debacle that put it in worse shape than Los Angeles, as far as the game of polo was concerned.

We had been living in Arizona for about a year. One day, while Carrie was visiting her parents in Albuquerque, I was driving around the hinterlands of Phoenix when I drove by an equestrian type place and noticed a Polo match taking place.

Ah, ha! At last!

Bob, the club's director between chukars let me know of his intent to sell a thoroughbred polo horse and invited me to play with them the next Friday. While not so interested in buying a horse, I was overwhelmed at finding living, breathing polo players. I exchanged telephone numbers with my newly found friend and promised to return that next Friday.

My only problem was that I was supposed to fly to Albuquerque on Friday to meet Carrie. After nearly a week of begging, pleading and groveling on the telephone, Carrie gave me the okey-dokey to play. I changed my reservations for a later flight out.

It was Friday, December 13, 1991. Although my grandmother was superstitious and tried teaching me how to counter bad luck, I never picked it up. Even if I was superstitious nothing was going to stand in my way of playing polo.

Ominously, there is a range of mountains that looms behind the polo grounds. They are called the Superstition Mountains.

It was 3:05 pm when I arrived. The horses were already saddled, but only my new buddy, Bob, and his wife were there. Bob said that no one else could make it and I didn't think anything about it. We exchanged pleasantries and he questioned me about my abilities and then explained the equipment he was using on his horses. He was using traditional Polo equipment on his horse but not on the horse he had tacked for me. Since he had learned to play polo from Will Rogers, one of the most famous players of all time, I figured he knew what he was doing. I had brought my equipment but in my anxiousness to play chose not to use it since the horse was ready to go.

We started off slow, kind of leapfrogging each other and hitting the ball forward to each other. Within fifteen minutes of getting started my saddle twisted on the horse while at a canter and I fell off. I had never fallen from a horse before. Fear of being hurt or killed had kept me glued to the horse all this time. I rolled on the soft grass and was up on my feet, neither shaken nor stirred. I was amazed that it didn't hurt. It was a first for me, an accident with no bruises, cuts, or broken bones.

Bob brought the horse back to me. The horse, Jetta, hadn't fared as well. It seems the reigns had caught on the right stirrup and had scared the already extremely high-strung animal. Every time I tried to get back up on the horse it shied away from me. After about ten minutes, Jetta cautiously allowed me to climb aboard. We walked around the field for a few minutes to become reacquainted. When we resumed play the horse shied away from the ball each time we approached. This was upsetting to the rider. You see, when a horse is running and the rider is leaning out of the saddle to the right and the horse suddenly darts left, the affects of centrifugal force is reversed. The more Jetta did this, the more shaken my confidence was becoming.

Finally Jetta decided that he had enough of me, and playing polo and was going to take his toys and go home. Either that or Jetta thought it was time to play rodeo. It is impossible for me to describe the emotions behind what it feels like to be riding a horse at 35 miles an hour while it is bucking.

Kendrick taught me that in order to slow down a horse you turn it into a circle because it cannot run as fast. Surprisingly, no one had ever bothered to tell Jetta this fact. The tighter the circle, the faster we spun. At one point we were traveling so fast that I think we passed ourselves at least twice. I was starting to get a sick tummy and decided I wanted off this ride.

Every time I tried falling off Jetta, he felt the shift in my body weight and changed course. Amazing. Now I couldn't even fall off a horse when I wanted. In my efforts to eject, the saddle slipped again so when Jetta leapt to the left my saddle twisted all the way to the right. Jetta tried to get back under my weight but the force threw me off. I fell off the left side of the horse and did a kind of cartwheel in mid air before landing on the right side of my neck and shoulder. I bounced, skidded a few times, and then crumpled to the ground.

When I awoke, several minutes had passed. I was lying on my back and could see that Bob and his wife were off their horses and leading them over to me. As I sat up the world began spinning awkwardly and I was overcome with nausea. It took a few minutes but I noticed that my right shoulder was sitting in my lap, which seemed odd since I was never a limber person. Bob leaned over to give me a hand up by taking hold of my right hand and pulling. I let out a kind of high-pitched "ouch" and grabbed my arm away from Bob using my left hand. I slowly looked up and said that something was wrong. Bob looked at me in disbelief and told me that I just needed to get up and "walk it off." After slowly making my way to my feet, by myself, I shuffled over to where the vehicles were parked. I was shuffling because neither of my legs were working too well. My right knee no longer wanted to bend and my left ankle really smarted. Although it was only about 100 yards away, it looked like I might not make it before nightfall and might need to camp out along the way.

When we finally reached my car we stood there talking for a few minutes. I kept telling Bob that I wasn't feeling well and he kept telling me stories of the old days. Bob told me about how he got a glass eye after being kicked in the face by a horse. Then there was the time when he was hit in the face with a polo mallet that resulted in him getting a glass jaw. It was at this point I started questioning whether I should have gone out to play polo with this guy. I'm sure his stories were well meant but they didn't instill much solace in me, given the amount of pain I was experiencing. I finally asked Bob if he would either drive me to the hospital or call an ambulance.

While Bob finished getting the horses and the equipment back in the trailer, his wife Betty drove me, in my jeep, to the hospital. She let me out at the emergency entrance and then joined me in the waiting room. When the front desk person called me to register it was difficult to say anything because it seemed that if I attempted to speak I would burst out crying.

When a nurse came to take me back to the examining room Betty came right along with us. The nurse was going to cut off my boots and pants but when I refused Betty offered to help take them off. Between Betty and the nurse they were able to pry off my boots. The nurse left and told Betty to help me remove my pants. I stood and leaned back against the table as Betty unzipped my pants and pulled them down to my ankles. Although I wasn't in the best frame of mind, the humor of the situation was not lost on me. Here was this old lady, who I didn't even know, crouched down in front of me sliding my pants down. When I started to laugh Betty looked up at me like I was nuts.

As I lay in the hospital bed, in between x-rays and examinations, I tried calling my wife to let her know I wouldn't be arriving in Albuquerque but there was no answer at my in-laws' house. I tried calling my family but my parents weren't at home and my brother was at work but unavailable. I called my office but everyone had already gone home for the evening. Finally, I was able to get hold of my older sister, Kathy, and asked her to find Carrie and let her know what was happening.

Kathy made one telephone call. It was to a department store in one of the Malls. Call it women's intuition, but as soon as the store paged Carrie over the loud speaker she was just walking into the store. Carrie tried calling the hospital but I was already gone.

It turns out that the impact broke my right collar bone, both sternoclavicular joints (where the collar bones connect to the rib cage), and spinal stenosis in my neck. The hospital was booked solid for the evening so, after wrapping and strapping my body parts back to their general locations, I was released. Betty drove me home while Bob followed. We swung through the McDonalds drive-through for a Happy Meal and then to the drug store for some Happy Pills for dessert. Betty and Bob helped me into my house and propped me on the couch since there was no way to make it to the second floor and a bedroom.

By this time it was after midnight and all the frantic telephone calls I made earlier were paying off. Everyone was returning my telephone calls. Unfortunately we did not yet own a cordless telephone and I couldn't even try to get to the telephone. Not being able to reach me, a colleague came to the house to check my condition. He got the telephone with the extension cord from the bedroom and ran to the grocery store and returned with enough Gatoraid and Fig Newtons to carry me through an entire winter.

Carrie was finally able to get through to me at about 1:30 am. I told her not to worry, that the immense damage to my body and soul were mere scratches and I would survive to live a semi-normal life, if God was really, really on my side. The next morning at around 6:00 am after sleeplessly hallucinating all night I telephoned Carrie and told her to come home, I had lied and God was not on my side.

It was noon when a key hit the lock and Carrie came through the door. My boss, Terry, had picked Carrie up at the airport.

By this point, rigor mortis had set in and I could no longer turn my head and talking was painful. My leg was propped up on a chair and I was surrounded by pillows that held me in position. My right arm was in a sling and a harness held my shoulder in place.

Carrie could only exclaim, "What in the heck happened to you?"

I thought I had pretty much explained everything to her the previous evening and summed it up for her as, "Well, I was thrown from a horse!"

Being thrown from a horse sounds so much more macho than say, falling from a horse. Hearing of someone being thrown from a horse instantly brings to mind a vicious bucking bronco in a rodeo. Conversely falling from a horse denotes a vision of some incompetent boob sliding off the side of an old nag that is standing still eating a clump of hay. Therefore, I preferred to be thrown from my horse, thank you very much.

Terry, for his part, studied me very carefully and said, "I hope you don't plan on missing any work because of this darn foolish behavior."

I have to admit to you that Terry's language was a bit more colorful than this but you get the gist of it. This was probably the maddest I've ever been and it was a good thing that I couldn't talk or throw heavy objects.

On Monday it took me four hours to get showered and dressed but I made it into work. The Human Resource department had anticipated my arrival and had a wheel chair brought in for me but I hobbled around with a cane.

Within a few months of the accident, I had gone to enough doctors to choke a horse. Although, there was only one particular horse I wanted to choke.

Being a doctor sure is an interesting occupation. I was referred to several specialists through my HMO's general practitioner. A general practitioner is an interesting case study.

The name implies that these physicians have a general understanding about medical stuff. I'm one who believes that when I go to the doctor they should have a thorough understanding about medical stuff.

Unfortunately there are no "Thorough Practitioners" listed in the telephone book. There are a lot of specialists though. The problem with specialists is that they don't seem too concerned about medical problems outside their field of expertise. For example, I went to an orthopedic surgeon for one problem and when I told him about another problem he told me that I'd have to see another specialist.

Nowadays I'm concerned that doctors have become like the three blind men trying to describe an elephant from a very specific vantage point. One guy feels the trunk and pronounces that an elephant is like a snake. Another guy feels a leg and pronounces that an elephant is like a tree. The last guy feels the side of the stomach and pronounces that an elephant is like a whale. It's no wonder that it ended up taking several years before I recovered.

There's an old adage that if you fall off a horse, you've got to get right back on. Whoever thought of that one had to be a complete lunatic. If you ever fall off a horse, turn away and keep on walking, especially if it's Friday the 13th.

Hobnobbing in Hollywood

Living in Los Angeles afforded Carrie and I the ability to appreciate the mysteries of Hollywood.

When we were bored and in search of something to do, we would drive from our apartment in Burbank around the hill to Hollywood - a city of paradoxes, a place where opposites attract. We loved to watch the diversity of people. Hollywood is definitely a city of fruits and nuts.

Hollywood Boulevard is where the tourists and street beggars hang out. Back then the corner of Hollywood and Vine was just a bunch of dirty and dilapidated old buildings that appeared to be vacant. One evening we drove by a nightclub that had a line of people waiting to gain entrance that extended an entire city block. There were police cars and ambulances parked in front and to our amazement a person in a body bag lay on the sidewalk in front of the entrance. The people waiting in line just walked around the dead person like it was nothing.

Sunset Strip was where the prostitutes and their clientele hung out. I believe at least one famous movie star was caught in the act with a woman of ill repute in a parked car in broad daylight. Sunset also had some great comedy clubs and infamous bars where rock groups often get their break.

Melrose Boulevard was a place of black clothing. Whether you were new age, generation-X, yuppie types in BMW's or bikers on Harleys, everyone was dressed in all black clothing. It was interesting to see these two distinct groups of people sitting at sidewalk cafes. The chic right next to dirty and disheveled. Talk about living on the edge.

We regularly visited Fred Segal's, a clothing store, on Melrose. The clientele ranged from young women in jeans to the very rich elite. In the parking lot we would see a beat up old Volkswagen Bug parked next to a Rolls Royce, although limousines outnumbered any other type of car. Segal's kept only one of each size of clothing on the racks and on one occasion I was trying on suits, black of course, and ended up switching back and forth with Harry Hamlin who was getting outfitted for a Tonight Show appearance. On another occasion I was shopping for ties and we literally bumped into Madonna. She was wearing blue jeans and wore no make-up. For the next two hours she and Carrie talked while they picked out my ties. Madonna seemed like just a regular person and I have to say is one of the nicest people I have ever met.

As a result of playing polo, attending polo matches and living on the fringe of polo culture, we had an opportunity to meet some interesting people. Without a doubt the highest concentration of television and movie stars we met were at the LA Equestrian Center's professional polo matches. There were polo players who were television personalities, rock musicians, and even an operatic singer. They were regular people who were fun to be around. Unlike most team sports that I've participated in, very few of these guys threw a hissy fit if someone goofed up out on the field. I'll admit there might have been one or two guys who were strung a little too tightly.

A week before being accused of slapping a policeman, Zsa Zsa Gabor had thrown out the first ball at a Polo match. As she was leaving with her entourage I was walking past when she leaned over and clipped my shoulder. Given that she had the weight advantage it felt like I had been hit by a linebacker and the impact spun me around. She didn't apologize or even acknowledge my existence. My shoulder hurt for a week.

On our many trips to Santa Barbara to watch the polo matches we had an opportunity to meet some very famous people. The person who stands out most in my mind is Sylvester Stallone. This guy had his own Polo team in Hawaii that occasionally played at Santa Barbara. He was a nice enough guy and I liked him a lot, but you could tell he was trying too hard to seem intelligent and witty, like he was fighting against the image created by some of his movies. I have never been around a person who used so many multi-syllabic words in every sentence. Afterwards I must have spent hours looking at the dictionary to make sure I hadn't made a fool of myself.

However, many of the famous people we met were snobbish and arrogant. Carrie and I were in agreement that if these folks didn't acknowledge our existence then we weren't going to talk to them either.

I learned a most valuable lesson when we took my wife's cousin to a polo match. She wanted Alan Thicke's autograph so we walked over and asked. From that point on he never spoke to me again. Granted that could have been because he didn't know me or perhaps knew me only too well. I came to realize that these people probably don't have many real friends, just people who want something from them. After all, a star is just a person above all else, and as such, probably values unconditional friendship even more than most of us.

I personally don't like it when people feign friendship in order to get something from me. What is most disconcerting is that disingenuous people think you're too dumb to know they are trying to use you.

Rather than look at these folks as being elite and unapproachable, I chose to look at them in a different light. Sure, they are rich and famous beyond my wildest dreams. Of course I'll never be an equal or even remotely in their league. But they are just people with hopes and dreams who put their pants on one leg at a time. Some of them are good and some are bad just like in the real world.

It just so happens these folks are good at their jobs, for the most part, and get much more visibility than the regular Joe. Celebrity and fame doesn't mean they're any smarter or more competent or better than anyone else though.

A New Life

It was about 2:00 pm on a sweltering August day at our home in Arizona when I received a telephone call at work from Carrie. She had just returned from a doctor appointment and sounded sullen and uneasy. The doctor told her she might be pregnant. Previously we had discussed having children only in the broadest sense, always in the terms of "someday." I have always loved other people's children. It was fun to get the kid all worked up and then leave the parents to suffer after the kid was in full melt down.

Having a sister, Dannielle, ten years younger than I, had fully prepared me for having children. Whenever my parents would go out to dinner, shopping or whatever, I would baby-sit. At least in my mind that's the way it worked out. While, at first, Dannielle tested my limits and childcare ability, we soon reached an agreement for when my parents were not around. I deny all her claims that I tied her to a chair until she had eaten dinner. It was, after all, belts that I used. Besides, eating the required amounts from each of the four food groups is important. Although, I generally ate candy bars for sustenance in those days.

When Carrie told me that she thought she was pregnant, I was instantly overcome by a feeling of exhilaration I had never experienced in my 31 years. I was so happy that I was speechless. A first time event. Carrie was mortified and she took my silence as confirming her suspicions that I was upset with her. Carrie cried as she delivered the news. I had always supposed that the reason we didn't have any children yet was that we weren't sure if the marriage was going to last. After ten years of marriage I wasn't sure if she was crying because she thought she was pregnant or if she was crying at the thought of it being part of me.

When we arrived home from work that evening, we sat and discussed what the doctor had said. When would we know for sure? Carrie had taken a pregnancy test but the results wouldn't be ready until the following week. The thought of going through the weekend not knowing was excruciating. We went to the grocery store and purchased a home pregnancy test. Carrie procrastinated for a few days until I had to insist she take the test. I really had to know. The home pregnancy test was negative. We weren't pregnant. By this time we had both built up expectations that we wanted a child. All hope was not lost. We would get the final results from the doctor, which could come back positive. We waited. Two days later, Carrie received a call at work from the doctor. We were not pregnant.

At home that night we talked about having a baby. We talked about our hopes and fears. My fears involved how a baby would look just like us and take on our good traits and our bad traits. I figured any child that "wore" my genes was at a great disadvantage.

After that night neither of us discussed having a baby for a few weeks. At that time, we both thought about it so much, it was hard for us to talk at all. It seemed that life would never be the same. Finally, we began hinting to one another about having children. Just seeing new parents in the mall took on a whole new meaning.

Even though her job was new and my job was no longer any fun, we decided that it would never be the right time to start a family. So, we had to make up our minds and just do it. Carrie assured me that if she hadn't left me in the first ten years of our marriage there was at least a good 50/50 chance we'd make it another ten years.

Becoming a family would be a nice change. It couldn't be that bad, after all I raised my little sister all by myself. Carrie had a mother's instinct when she was six and adopted a purple colored baby chicken, appropriately named Chicky. It was Easter time when Carrie got Chicky and she raised it to adulthood as a single parent. Of course, like most children, Chicky flew the coop. Actually, it was sent to boarding school at her uncle's ranch. Her parenting skills were called into question one Sunday dinner at the ranch when her cousin, Jacque, exclaimed, "Guess who were having for dinner?"

By January 1993, we had been practicing fairly regularly and there was a chance she was finally pregnant. We stopped by the corner drug store and got a couple of their best home pregnancy tests. She refused to tell me the results. How cruel is that? After rummaging through the bathroom, I found the test. Upon removing the test from its hiding place, I promptly spilled it all over myself. I have to admit that, for a few minutes, I forgot about the pregnancy thing until I had cleaned myself off. These home pregnancy tests are so gross when you think about it. The indicator had changed color and we were pregnant. I tried not to be too optimistic since the line was red and not bright red like the instructions said it should be for a positive result. My heart couldn't take it if it weren't true. Carrie and I waited anxiously throughout the following days until she could get confirmation through her doctor. After finding out the good news, I instantly became terrified. What on earth had we gone and done this time?

Every night before bed Carrie and I would lay down on the couch with me positioned to read humorous stories to her stomach. I knew the baby would have a good sense of humor because he would really move around during the funny parts.

A few months into her pregnancy Carrie began having problems that were a cause for worry and created many sleepless nights. For Easter, we traveled to Carrie's hometown outside Albuquerque to visit her parents. Carrie was over five months pregnant and it wouldn't be too long before we couldn't travel until after the baby was born. Carrie had a wonderful time with her mom that weekend. Her mom, Flora, had already done quite a bit of shopping and had begun assembling heirlooms for our baby. She had found a picture of a toddler, that she envisioned would look and act like our child, who had gotten carried away with unraveling several rolls of tissue paper in the bathroom. Throughout our visit, the look on Flora's face expressed concern about the well being of her daughter and the baby.

The first night after returning home to Phoenix we were awakened at 3:25 am by the telephone. Carrie's brother was calling to inform us that Flora had just passed away in her sleep. Carrie took the news very hard and we became even more concerned about her and the baby.

The night before the funeral I was surprised when Carrie's family asked me to deliver the Eulogy. Flora and I had a stereotypical in-law-type of relationship. We bugged each other. Since we were such opposites, I couldn't rely on my own experiences with Flora so I got each family member to reminisce. Rather than be solemn I chose to talk about Flora's character as a practical joker and storyteller. Throughout the process I learned that she and I were a lot alike, although my stories are much better.

I've always taken comfort in Flora's passing by believing that her love for Carrie was so great that she somehow sacrificed her life in order to ensure Carrie and our child were healthy. It's one of those inexplicable things that happen. Although, I'm still afraid of her even in death.

On learning the sex of our child we chose a name for him, Christian Taylor. We just liked the name. The due date was anticipated for late August, the same day as my 90-year-old grandmother's birthday.

In the weeks leading up to the due date I kept telling Carrie that she'd had him long enough and that it was now my turn. Being her stubborn self she refused to give him up to me.

We had long since given up our second floor bedroom because Carrie couldn't waddle up the stairs. We slept on the twin bed in the spare bedroom. Finally, one Sunday night at 11:00 pm, Carrie tried to wake me up. Her water, whatever that means, broke and I needed to get her to the hospital. In my sleepiness I thought she was telling me that she was getting out of bed for some water so I kept going back to sleep. When the bedroom door slammed shut I knew something was up and jumped into my clothes and shot out the door to get the car. We arrived at the airport in minutes. Why exactly I had driven to the airport I don't know, but we managed to make good time from there to the hospital.

Carrie's labor was fairly quick, only seven or eight hours. There was a chair in the room that converted to a bed. It was a little difficult to get much sleep though because nurses kept coming in to check on Carrie. Besides Carrie was always asking for ice water or some such thing. I'm sure her attitude was that if she couldn't sleep, I wasn't going to sleep either. Delivery on the other hand was long, slow, and painful. I'm not sure what Carrie thought of it though. I was wishing we had one of those "30 minutes or it's free" kind of deals like pizza delivery restaurants offer. Carrie's labor was quick as compared to the delivery, which lasted over 14 hours. For a while I thought she was going to have a pony.

About five hours into it, the doctor began medicating to control her blood pressure. It would swing high and then very low. At some points she became delirious. One time she told me that I'd better leave to get some socks and a new tie for the cat. I knew she was delirious if only because our cat is a casual dresser and doesn't care for formalwear of any kind.

The baby had begun coming through the birth canal and got stuck. The doctor was having an increasingly difficult time controlling Carrie's blood pressure. The baby was becoming increasingly distressed as time progressed. Because the baby was so far down the birth canal a C-section was out of the question. About 12 hours into the delivery, the doctor asked to talk with me outside the room. He discussed the problems and alluded to me having to make choices concerning Carrie and the baby. I remember being very calm but I don't recall what I had said. I do know that I was firm in my position that there would be no choices because he was going to get whatever help he needed to make sure everything worked out okay. Carrie's delivery room quickly filled with doctors and nurses who poked, prodded and pulled until the baby came out. Two doctors took him to an area in the corner of the room and began work right away on checking him out. The baby had a blue tint to his skin and didn't cry. His eyes were open and as I talked to him he looked around for my voice. Within a few minutes they were taking him down the hall.

I looked to the doctors working on Carrie and asked if she was going to be okay. When they said yes, I was out the door and following Christian down the hallway. I questioned the doctor about his health and he said that it would be 24 hours before they'd know for sure. When they were done, I sat there holding Christian in my arms through the night. A few times I'd run down the hall and check on Carrie just to make sure she was okay too.

Much to the chagrin of our HMO, Carrie and Christian spent a few days in the hospital. The day before checking out, the doctor came to perform the circumcision. This is the only medical procedure that Christian has ever undergone without me being present. There's something about getting a sensitive body part cutoff that gives me the heebie-jeebies. I stood just outside the door of the little operating room and waited for the blood-curdling scream, but it never came. After about fifteen minutes a nurse came out and said the procedure was complete and that the baby didn't make a peep.

As I waited for them to bring Christian from the operating room I hear the most intense scream I had ever heard in my life. I rushed into the operating room and demanded to know what was going on. A nurse looked up at me and said the baby just pooped and began to laugh. At this point I was quite assured that my worst fears were going to be realized. Christian was going to be just like me. Sadly though, he quickly outgrew the childish antics that have taken me my whole life to perfect.

While I didn't get a pony, I did get a monkey, one that climbs and hangs from everything imaginable.

An Introduction to Mountaineering

While on a family vacation at Banff National Park in the Rocky Mountains of Alberta, Canada, I, for some unknown reason, decided to take a lesson in rock climbing. Though I'm sure that Carrie had something to with it. A local sporting goods store in Banff provided a one-and-a-half hour class for $15 dollars right inside the store. There were two other people taking the class, recent college graduates from Australia who had been traveling around North America in a van for the past eight months.

Until this point I had never really considered myself as being old. My mind remembered that my body could once do one-armed pull-ups and push-ups. Unfortunately my body was suffering from a bad case of Alzheimer's and couldn't remember a thing, although my mind and body don't generally get along during the best of times.

My Australian friends would shimmy right to the top. The show offs. It was a little humiliating each time I fell off the simulated rock face. The store's patrons, who gathered to watch, would either cringe or laugh as I struggled against gravity. It might not have been so bad if I were able to actually get both feet off the floor before falling. Apparently the exchange rate between the two countries also impacts the gravitational force. One pound in the U.S. seemed to weigh 1.5 pounds in Canada. I assume my feet had something to do with my not being able to climb but couldn't really see them to know for sure. It wasn't that I was out of shape it's just that my shape had rounded.

After having suffered numerous indignities that day, I committed myself to regaining the ground I had lost since my last athletic pursuit. I made a personal vow to try again and the next time I didn't want to stink at the sport.

Upon returning to our home in Michigan I began my training by reading climbing magazines. Diving right in like that was probably a little too strenuous on my mind and body but I felt obligated to persevere. It's amazing how many types of climbing there are - rock climbing, bouldering, sport climbing, gym climbing, ice climbing, mountaineering, winter mountaineering. When I asked someone at a local store to explain the difference, they became incensed that I could be so ignorant. Convenience store clerks can be so rude.

Gym climbing was interesting and I tried it out for quite awhile. Since I had taken a Physics class in college I was aware of the law of gravity and the fact that it made me unable to climb any overhang. Besides, I didn't want to be arrested for violating such a basic law.

Having a lifelong dream of becoming a mountain man, like Robert Redford in the movie about Jeremiah Johnson, I felt compelled to pursue mountaineering as the closest modern day activity. It wasn't surprising to me that I would sign-up for a multi-day mountaineering course. My wife was impressed with my restraint. Under normal circumstances she would have expected that I would have signed up to climb Mt. Everest once I discovered I was so talented in rock climbing.

One day while busily doing research on the Internet I stumbled across a seven day introductory mountaineering course offered in Banff National Park. This was a perfect opportunity to return to the scene of the crime and prove my mettle. The course would take us into the backcountry, across glaciers, and up mountains.

There was only one slight problem, I had only camped outside one night during my entire life. It was a winter Boy Scout camping trip to Georgetown Lake, 25 miles west of Anaconda, my hometown. We had trekked across the frozen lake covered with a few feet of snow to the scout leaders cabin. The cracking and popping of the ice had me scared to

An Introduction to Mountaineering   85

death. Once we reached his cabin we pitched large canvas tents, each one holding eight to ten kids. My cotton sleeping bag did little to keep me warm and I put on all the clothes I had brought along.

When I was even younger I attempted sleeping outside with my friends but some catastrophic problem always seemed to occur that would result in our aborting the adventure. Namely darkness. As soon as darkness would descend upon us, some strange crackle or crunch would send my friends and I ricocheting off the fence, clothesline and trees until reaching the safety of the backdoor where we would casually and quietly enter the house and make our way to the bedroom to complete the sleepover. We weren't afraid of the dark, we just had an aversion to the eerie things that stalked us in the dark.

Since I had a few months to get ready for the mountaineering course I carefully constructed a rigorous exercise plan. It involved regular aerobic activity and weight training. Unfortunately, a few months is a really long time to stay focused, especially when every muscle is aching from lactic acid overload and years of neglect. I managed to sustain my effort for the first two weeks of the plan. A job change from Michigan to Texas disrupted my routine, not that I would intentionally look for disruptions to end my pain and suffering, mind you. Suffice it to say my physical abilities would not be at peak performance in time for the course.

The thing that probably attracted me most to mountaineering is the diversity of gear and gadgets that are available, such as ascenders, belay devices, boots, carabiners, compass, crampons, harness, ice screws, ice axes, rope, sleeping bags, tents, warm weather clothes, cold weather clothes, and freezing cold weather clothes. Don't get me wrong, I hate shopping as much as the next guy, but looking for gear and gadgets is just so cool. I got married so I didn't have to shop for clothes anymore. But then I learned about the level of technology used in mountaineering clothes - well it's like gadgets you can wear.

We all met at 8:30 am on August 23rd, at the guide's office for a briefing and equipment inspection. The guides rummaged through our ample stores of equipment. They checked mine out twice and I ended up leaving more behind than I was taking.

As I stood there in my brightly colored mismatching clothes and gear, my first thought was that I hoped no price tags were visibly hanging. My second observation was that all the other climbers were able to carry their backpack with one hand. This struck me as odd. They must have trained very hard since I was barely able to shoulder my backpack by myself.

Everyone commented on how new my boots looked. I'd had the boots for a few weeks already so they weren't really new, new. Although breaking them in consisted of wearing them on weekends in town, shopping, and mowing the lawn. They seemed quit comfortable and I was pleased with their snug fit.

At 10:00 am we drove 40 miles to Lake Louise and met at Laggan's bakery and coffee shop. It seems there is a tradition dating back to when the land was being explored to stop at Laggan's. After about an hour of sitting on the curb and eating pastries we drove another half hour to the Num-Ti-Juh Lodge at Bow Lake. There, each of us received a portion of the group's food to carry. The guides checked some of our backpacks again, and spent some quality time adjusting mine so it would fit properly. By noon, after fiddling with backpacks and sunscreen, we were off.

The Internet is a great place to find information about weather, trail conditions and the like. This is not necessarily a good thing. I kept coming across trail reports about grizzly bear activity. I refuse to have my plans dictated by grizzly bears, but I am open to any suggestions they may have. What I finally settled on was partnering with another climber who was older, slower, and in worse physical condition than myself. This way, should we encounter a grizzly bear, I could out run my companion who would serve to "slow" the bear down for my get-away. As it turned out, this was a common objective shared by all the climbers.

I'm not usually a talkative, effervescent, and popular person in social settings but these folks seemed to sense my natural abilities and in turn each asked if they could partner with me during the trek through the forest.

There were 18 clients and three guides, broken into three groups made up of six clients and a guide. The selection was based on whoever was ready to go at the time. Each group traveled about 30 minutes apart to avoid the congestion of one large group.

In my group was Brad, an engineer from Great Falls, Montana; Doug, a professional photographer from Halifax, Nova Scotia; and three women. Sue was a college student from British Columbia, and was on sabbatical - taking a tour of the country in her van. She had just landed a summer job studying the morphology of glaciers. Jennifer is a PhD Engineer. She was tall, very slender, and I was quite intimidated by her. The weekend prior to our course Jennifer had competed in a 24-hour mountain bike race in the Kokanee mountains. Laura worked for a major shoe and clothing manufacturer and every visible piece of her clothing carried an emblem – she was a walking billboard. I was afraid to take photographs of Laura as I might infringe upon a copyright law.

I read a magazine article recently in which the author said something to the effect, "When you take an infinite number of items that are infinitely light, you create something infinitely heavy." This is a physical law that you cannot fully appreciate until about two hours of backpacking. It doesn't matter if you're on flat ground or a steep incline, it's heavy. Some enterprising person would do well to set up shop along mountain trails where they'd be able to buy brand new gear for just pennies.

I was able to learn this lesson painlessly when the guides pared my load prior to taking off from the trailhead. Thereafter, this lesson was reinforced every second I struggled under the ever increasing weight of my load. I considered giving away gadgets and clothing to hikers we passed on the trail; cutting labels from clothing and breaking my toothbrush in half were certainly on the list too.

I'd never had blisters on my feet before so I was really caught off guard when within 15 or 20 minutes of passing the trailhead my feet, glowing red, became visible through my boots. Wisps of smoke escaped, smelling of burning hamburger. I hated those boots and they were way too tight.

Our first day consisted of hiking several kilometers from the trailhead to Bow hut, about 3,000 vertical feet. Although, the trail winds up and down the northern side of Crowfoot Mountain way too many times. The hike crossed a glacier-fed creek several times until we hiked above the tree line. Two hours above tree line we stopped for a rest and the guide, Mike, pointed up into the sky to the top of a ridge and a small dot. Apparently the hut was the size of a thimble. It was at the top of the ridge. We were at the bottom of a valley and the walls seemed vertical. The hump to the hut was exhausting. My lungs were being sucked out of my chest with every breath. We finally reached the hut. The good new was that we were just in time for dinner. The bad news was that we had to cook dinner. I have problems boiling water at sea level so I was really looking forward to dinner.

An Introduction to Mountaineering 89

By 10:00 pm we had finished cleaning up the dishes and were all stacked snugly into our sleeping bags. I was really looking forward to sleeping because I was completely bushed. I put in my ear plugs and promptly lay there listening to my heart trying to beat its way out of my chest. Sometime during the night, unable to sleep, my brain decided to hallucinate. My sleeping bag magically turned into a raft and I was floating in the ocean, fishing for brook trout with my light fly rod and tackle.

We all struggled out of our sleeping bags around 6:30 am. It turns out that very few of us had slept.

We were set to go out onto the Wapta glacier and climb a mountain known as the "Onion Skin" because it resembles a large onion showing the many layers. As we began getting ready it started raining so we spent an hour or so inside the hut learning and practicing knots and hitches. Once the rain stopped we strapped on our harness and crampons and made our way onto the glacier. We learned the delicate job of walking in crampons without maiming others or ourselves and practiced the fine art of front pointing and using our ice ax to climb out of deep crevasses.

After lunch we learned crevasse rescue techniques to retrieve a fallen climber. Each of us also was lucky enough to play the victim by being lowered into the bowels of a deep blue, freezing cold and scary crevasse. I was delighted when we returned with no severed arteries and my pant legs in one piece.

The guide leading us this day was, John, a 58-year-old New Zealander, affectionately referred to as a "Kiwi." Not only is John an expert mountaineer, he is one of the toughest people I've ever met. When we arrived at the Bow Hut, he started doing fingertip pull-ups on the door jam. When no one was around I reached up to try for myself but only succeeded in cracking the door jam. I think that John was a very likeable and sociable fellow but I'm not completely sure because with his accent, or mine, I couldn't understand a word he said.

Anytime we were harnessed and roped together John had a habit of asking, "Are you screwed up?"

After being asked this question several times I figured John suspected I was completely incompetent and was looking for me to confirm his suspicion. A few weeks after the course I came to a hopeful conclusion that he really wanted to know if my carabiner was screwed shut. In any case I was covered either way since I had always answered "yes" to his question.

The second night was much better, awakening only to answer the call of nature. Since nature is outside and it is very cold outside, it was a very brief visit. On this particular morning it was quite difficult to get out of my nice and cozy sleeping bag.

At 7:00 am, after choking down some very dry banana bread, we were on our way to the Peyto hut, an elevation of 8,200 feet. This day had us traveling on the glacier several kilometers past the "Onion Skin," to climb 10,900 foot Mount Rhonda before descending to the hut that lay on the opposite side of the glacier. While I expected that my body would begin to acclimatize to the altitude, my breathing consisted of hyperventilating.

I was once again with John's group.

Every time I asked, "Are we there yet?"

His reply was, "Fifteen minutes."

I swear, his watch had to be broken. The man had no sense of time.

Finally I changed my modus operandi and asked, "How far before we rest again?"

His response became, "50 meters."

That was a pretty good tactic on his part because by the time I converted 50 meters into feet we had gone well past it. The man had no sense of distance.

There is a small glacial lake about 400 vertical feet from the hut that had to be traveled because it was our only source of water. There's nothing like the taste of greenish water, heavy on the sand, to take your thirst away.

During our third night there was a thunderstorm that lasted all night. A heavy fog rolled into the valley and we were in a total whiteout until after 10:00 am. Once the fog lifted we headed off to an unnamed peak the local climbers call "My Way Peak," perched next to Mount Baker on the border of Alberta and British Columbia. Mike was our guide and our goal was to begin learning route-finding skills. He was very patient as we crisscrossed the glacier, in our attempt to approach and ascend from the backside of the mountain. At one point we happened upon an impassable crevasse and had to back track for another route. The alternate route required that we cross a narrow bridge of ice that spanned a 20-foot crevasse that was so dark it seemed bottomless. The first route seemed bad and I was convinced that the alternate route was going to kill us.

On the opposite side of the crevasse the solid ice slope was at an incline of 50+ degrees. Mike ended up taking all of our ice axes to establish anchors on both sides of the crevasse, climbed up the slope to a rocky outcropping and established a belay station. One by one we slowly made our way across the crevasse and then front pointed with our crampons to the safety of boulders and scree - loose rock chips collecting along the mountains slopes.

To get a view of where we needed to climb next we proceeded up the boulder field to the top of the rock outcropping. Rather than keep taking our crampons on and off every time we encountered some rock we left them on. As we climbed my right foot slipped down between two large rocks causing me to lose my balance. My body twisted while I tried to catch my balance but my foot stayed solidly anchored between the rocks.

I felt a fleeting but sudden and sharp pain shoot up through my leg, like a jolt of lightening. I continued climbing. The top of My Way Peak was about an hour away and we reached it without further incident.

After taking photographs we began descending along a different trail that passed down a steep snowfield and across a snowless glacier. My knee took the brunt of the constant grinding and pounding from descending the hard ice and it really started to be a bother. The route off the mountain was much less challenging than the ascent but the angle of descent and hardness of the glacial ice just wasn't a good combination. Traveling downhill meant we were going at a quick and steady pace. Not wanting to make a fuss, I tried to keep the whimpering to myself and only stopped the group for an occasional breather.

Within two and a half kilometers of reaching the hut it was all I could do to even walk. Luckily we were able to un-rope and I was able to travel at a more moderate (extra slow) pace. Within a kilometer I had to slow my pace to a near shuffle like a decrepit old man.

Even though I think that I have a fairly high pain threshold after all I've been through over the years, my knee was really hurting.

After what seemed like years, I finally reached the hut and loaded up on Ibuprofen. My knee was badly swollen and the joint had become so stiff that I couldn't bend my knee without a good deal of pain. Putting weight on my leg was no longer an option. We were about 16 kilometers from the trailhead and 50 kilometers away from civilization.

That night I had a fitful sleep and the next morning my situation hadn't improved. Not wanting to be a complete wimp I thought I could walk off the stiffness and pain by hiking down the hill to the lake in order to fill my water bottle. The pain was so intense I couldn't even make it past the side of the hut.

I met with Mike and John and the decision was made. Mike called for a rescue helicopter. I was devastated. All the effort I expended to get this far, only to see it end the day before the course was finished.

John had taken the group out onto the glacier for the trek back to Bow Hut. Mike stayed with me until the helicopter arrived. A park warden hopped from the helicopter, put a splint on my leg and then carried me over to the helicopter. I was really saddened as we flew over the glacier and past the group.

Once reaching Banff, the park warden took me by jeep to the Mineral Springs Hospital.

After being released from the hospital, I called home to Carrie. We had been married fifteen years by now and not many words were needed. Carrie knew just by the fact that it was day six of the seven-day course that something bad had happened.

It wasn't all bad though: I got to experience the thrill of flying in a helicopter through the rugged majesty of the Canadian Alps. I was able to try out the Canadian healthcare system for myself. It wasn't all that bad, but it was fairly expensive. Thankfully there was a favorable currency exchange rate.

Much to my wife's chagrin, every telephone cord, rope, strap, or appliance cord in our home is either in a Skein or a Mountaineers' coil.

Mt Shafer: Youth Is Wasted On The Young

It seems there is a direct correlation between one's level of physical fitness and the enjoyment derived from mountaineering. The more physically fit, the more enjoyable the experience. At least that's what I keep being told. Being a contrarian, it's my duty to try and prove them wrong.

There is a saying that, "Youth is wasted on the young." If only I'd known then what I should know by now. Not only did I find ignorance blissful in my youth, it seems to have followed me through life.

In an effort to actively pursue my youth through mountaineering, I hooked up with Jim, a certified mountaineering guide, based out of Golden, British Columbia. We planned a few days of mountaineering in western Alberta, culminating in a climb of Mt. Athabasca, seen from the Ice Fields Parkway between Banff and Jasper. It's reportedly a good peak for beginners. It was early July and the weather was a mite backwards, snowing almost every day. Thick, wet snow that, with each step, results in post-holing all the way up to your waist. In a word, not-much-fun.

Having invested my life's savings on this vacation, the change in plans was not welcome. Understood, but not welcome.

We decided to spend a day climbing on the crag at the end of Lake Louise, overlooking the beautiful turquoise water. The second day was spent climbing a route on Banff's Cascade Mountain called, "The Mother's Day Buttress." So named because some local kids spent the day rock climbing instead of with their mother's. This multi-pitch route, several hundred feet off the valley floor, was my most ambitious rock climb to date. After parking my rental car along a busy roadway we approached the base of the mountain through thick brush leading to even thicker forest. The vertical ascent of the climbing route is marked with good handholds but the rock is sharp, and quickly gnawed through my gloves.

About 600 feet up I made a horrific mistake. I looked down.

Climbing offers many challenges, but as one who is afraid of heights, none of them is greater than the fear of falling. As I peered out, the town of Banff looked especially tiny from my lofty perch. The cars whizzing past on the Trans-Canada highway looked like a line of ants racing back and forth with their picnic spoils.

As I resumed climbing I rediscovered spirituality and religion. Although I was never a real religious person, as a child I once dressed as a sheep for a Christmas play at the church. I hoped that counted for something. I suppose I'm not really afraid of falling just the trauma resulting from the sudden deceleration. The ground seems to get progressively harder the further one falls.

Having married a Catholic, I felt entitled to put the sign of the cross on my harness, the rope, and particularly tricky handholds.

My spirituality seemed to intensify as we moved further up the mountain and approached the crux, a slight overhanging rock. Feeling that my time on earth was limited, I repented every bad act that I, or anyone I'd known, had ever committed. I clarified that, as a young boy, I had only glanced at the ladies underwear section of the Sears & Roebuck catalog on my way to the hunting and fishing equipment, just in case there was any confusion.

By the time we reached the overhang I could have qualified for Sainthood.

I had to be careful not to let my fear cause me to enter into any binding contracts. I was already contractually prevented from participating in a number of sporting activities after being caught in some arduous jams. For his part, the "big guy" let me live and, for my part, I promised to take up a new sport. It was getting to the point that each new sport kept turning out to be even more dangerous than the previous one.

To get past the overhang I somehow had to maneuver myself underneath, to the side and then pull myself on top. As I clutched the top of the overhanging rock my legs swung freely out in space.

At this point I could have easily qualified as Pope.

Holding a hand-sized rock in my right hand, I couldn't help but admire its color, texture, and weight. I wondered how the rock formation was created, pushed from the earth so many eons ago. My thoughts were interrupted by the fact that I was now dangling from my left hand. The piece of rock, still in my right hand, had just moments before held me to the side of the mountain. It had broken away just as I was about to reach for a better handhold.

My options were to panic, panic, or panic. After careful consideration I chose to panic. This was good because even though the climb had already produced quite a bit of adrenaline in my system, the extra boost was just enough to get me over the edge.

Once I was safely to the top I licked my finger, not a smart thing to do after spending hours crawling up a rock face inhabited by rodents, and chalked an invisible mark in the air.

The next morning we packed our gear and headed out to Lake O'Hara, accessible only by foot or on a bus that runs twice daily. The lake is several kilometers from the main roadway, winding through the mountains on a one-lane dirt road. Near the end is a campground and at the end of the road is a fancy lodge for a few select well-to-do guests.

The whole week had been overcast and, by comparison, Banff now seemed like a tropical paradise. The spring thaw was just beginning to get underway and there was mushy snow and mud all around us. The wintry conditions meant increased grizzly bear activity at the lower levels. This meant that campsites have strict rules on food storage and preparation. The one benefit is that it was too cold for mosquitoes. I guess you can't have everything.

After setting our tents we immediately struck out to climb Mt. Shafer. A climb that involved trekking through soft snow for a few kilometers and climbing nearly vertical rock. As we approached the base of the route we could see a group of people silhouetted above us.

We surmised that because of their speed and colorful clothing, they were most probably some of the young folks who worked at the lodge. College students live and work at places like this during the summer, spending their day-off hiking and climbing. These kids are noted for their outstanding fitness and brevity.

Watching them climb, I could feel myself aging, especially as I struggled up the side of the mountain.

A few hundred feet from the summit we stopped for a water break. Upon fumbling with my backpack I promptly dropped my water bottle, watching it fall about fifty feet before catching in a cradle of rocks below. Jim and I looked at each other. He said that I probably needed my water bottle and I nodded agreement. For several minutes we both sat there looking down at where my water bottle had lodged.

Finally, Jim asked if I would like him to "run down and get it." I quickly accepted his gracious offer before he had a chance to reconsider.

As I took a sip of water I couldn't help but think how well it tasted. It was probably the best water I ever drank. Afterwards though, Jim didn't talk for the longest time.

Once on the summit, we sat and ate our lunch while looking at the unending views. Jim told me a harrowing experience of how he had survived a helicopter accident that past winter while heli-ski guiding. He had crushed a vertebrate in his back and had just recovered.

Usually only my mother could ever make me feel that guilty.

As we looked out over the valley we spotted a bear wading through the snow and decided it was time to get back to the campground. Since the bear was headed in our direction, we needed to move quickly.

By the time we neared the campground I was completely exhausted. My muscles were too tired to even throb with pain. Though they did moan rather loudly whenever I tried to move.

Safely off the mountain we stopped by the lodge for a quick refreshment. There is nothing like sitting next to a fireplace sipping hot chocolate on a cold July afternoon, complaining about one's ailments.

We struck up a conversation with one of the lodge employees and learned that the people climbing ahead of us were retirees. After coming off the mountain they went for a swim in the frigid lake waters and then hiked all the way back down to the trailhead.

Apparently youth is wasted on the young.

Father and Son Camping

My son, Christian, and I talked about taking our first camping trip for several months. It was two months before his seventh birthday and it seemed that this was the perfect age for our first father-son camping trip. I had just taken a new job and was commuting on the weekends between Dallas and Atlanta. While I'm sure that guilt played a role, I really wanted to spend some quality time with my son.

My father had been sick all during my childhood and we weren't able to do the outdoor thing. Complicated by the fact that there were five children vying for attention and I happened to be the maligned middle child. This was especially disappointing, since we lived along the edge of a massive wilderness area. The feeling seems akin to imprisoning an alcoholic in a liquor store, but not letting him drink.

So anyway, this was the first father-son camping trip for me too. I wasn't quite sure what to do, or how to go about doing it. But I knew we would work through it.

Prior to Christian being born, my wife and I had lived in Phoenix and spent all of our vacation time in Durango, Colorado. During Christian's lifetime however, we had only recently gone to visit our old haunt.

The week before we were to leave, Carrie found that she would not be able to go due to commitments at work. While her sudden loyalty to work caught me off guard, I reasoned that it could be plausible.

I'm not sure if it's a result of her or me getting older, but it seems that Carrie's true identity is slowly coming to light. You see, early in our marriage, we would frequently go into the backwoods to hike, fish and camp. Nowadays it seems that Carrie has metamorphosed into something I don't quite recognize. A home-cooked dinner is take-out ordered from a fancy sit-down restaurant. Camping is now roughing it at a four star hotel that uses real silverware and serves imported flavored coffee.

The sad thing is that she is warping the mind of our only child. I fear that without tough love or an "intervention" that Christian could fall prey to this depraved way of thinking. I wake up at night in a cold sweat after a nightmare that our son is... a city kid. Dear God, please, let it not be so.

So anyway, I decided that our first trip had to be something special. Someplace in the mountains. Someplace similar to where I could have gone as a child if my parents weren't giving all of their attention to my siblings and ignoring me. Christian and I spent a considerable amount of time planning this trip. Frankly, so long that I was fearful we would lose interest. Although for our next trip, we should discuss our plans before we pack, rather than at the airport while waiting to board the aircraft.

One bad trait that I picked up from my wife is spontaneity. The only thing we ever planned during our 18-year marriage is having a child. The only reason for that is because it takes nine months. On Carrie's due date, we got into an argument because I thought she was holding out on me and being selfish. I told her that since she hogged the baby for the first nine months, the second nine months he was all mine.

Okay, moving along here. Christian and I left Dallas on Wednesday and flew into Albuquerque. We rented a minivan and drove for what seemed like forever to Durango. Before leaving civilization, however, we stopped at a local outdoor store for provisions and fuel for our stove. Meals would consist of pull-string heat-em-up dinners. To appease Christian's gastronomical requirements we hit a convenience store and loaded up on soda, potato chips and candy bars. The basic food groups they teach you about in school.

I had been mountaineering for the past few years, but all of my camping was in rather harsh conditions above tree line or on glacial ice. I never really had to worry about wild things going bump in the night. After all, why would any self-respecting carnivore go traipsing into the middle of nowhere for a snack? Before we left home, Carrie had told me to take a gun, but it didn't really seem necessary.

I reasoned that we were not going to be camping more than a stones throw from civilization. Aside from squirrels and chipmunks, what animals want to be around human beings and all of their nasty habits? While Christian and I had discussions about the danger of guns, he had never seen a real gun and I did not want to frighten him or increase his curiosity.

We pulled into Durango at about three in the afternoon and took a quick cruise through town before heading out to the lake, about 25 miles from town. We drove to the farthest end of the lake to a small well-treed campground along the edge. The other campsites were spaced well enough from one another, so it seemed like the perfect place to pitch our tent. Rather than use the usual car camping gear I brought along my mountaineering equipment. I did leave behind things like ice axes, crampons, rope, carabiners and rock-climbing protection, but it was a difficult decision. A man does have to be concerned about overkill.

Setting the tent stakes was like trying to hammer into concrete. After the first stake was set, I had to move the whole tent because I didn't set it correctly and couldn't budge it. This memory would come back to haunt me later. Christian regularly offered assistance and direction. In fact, he was constantly climbing in and out of the tent and would even hang all over the delicate aluminum poles. Despite my fears, it seemed we now had the perfect equipment for car camping.

A few hours before sunset the park attendant stopped by to collect our fee and told me that a bear had been seen in the area a few nights before but hadn't been seen since. In any case, he said that it hadn't bothered anyone and the park rangers were vigilantly searching for it to keep tabs on its behavior. While this was somewhat alarming to me, I did take comfort in the fact that the animal had not bothered anyone and that the park attendant seemed rather unconcerned – telling me only to fulfill his park attendant obligation.

Taking heed of the possibility of attracting the bear, Christian and I decided that rather than risk smelling like food by cooking dinner at the campsite, we would drive halfway around the lake to a restaurant and eat hamburgers and chili. When we returned to the tent, Christian relaxed by playing his Gameboy. According to Christian, these electronic devices are critical camping equipment and quite possibly a legal requirement in some states. I tried reading a book, but for some reason, needed to sit and stare at my son and enjoy being with him.

Being a father is the best thing that ever happened to me.

Having a son that is so caring, smart and beautiful is truly heaven on earth. Eventually, his eyes wore out and I was able to persuade him to turn off that malevolent piece of electronic wonder.

We talked for the longest time about life. Important things, like why people poop and how he could build a nuclear reactor for a science project. Although I wasn't sure, it seemed as if Christian might have been trying to figure out how to build a nuclear reactor using poop. The inquisitive mind of youth is not something to be reckoned with. A Freudian psychologist would make a mint off of my family.

We fell asleep, with Christian in the nook of my shoulder, to the sound of light rain falling against the tent. A moment, one of many, that always comforts me.

When we awoke the next morning, the ground was fairly muddy from all of the rain during the night, so we were forced to drive into town and eat breakfast at McDonalds. We were tremendously disappointed to find that there is no breakfast happy meal. More specifically, Christian was bummed because they wouldn't give him one of those truly valuable toys. Given the number of these toys in Christian's toy box at home, we probably support a whole village of people somewhere in northern China and maybe even funded their nuclear weapons program. Who knows, they might even be using poop.

After eating our pancakes and sausage, we headed to a small lake about 20 miles in the opposite direction to do some fishing. We spent the majority of the day along the side of the lake reeling in some pretty hefty clumps of weeds. Sure there was an occasional rock, but we almost always lost them after setting the hook too quickly. We soon ran out of hooks and bait.

The elevation of that lake was about 10,000 feet above sea level. After a lunch of pull-string-to-heat chili, beef jerky and Cheetohs, we went on a hike toward Mt. Snowden, a 13,700 foot mountain. Within about 30 minutes Christian was tired, so I put him up on my shoulder to carry him. I say shoulder (singular) because Christian's legs always seem to fall asleep, like my neck is the size of a barrel or something. Gee whiz, what a wimp. There is nothing like the sound of a young child's high pitched whine, "Dad, I have picky's in my feet." Complaints that get repeated like a Thompson machine gun, just somewhat faster and more loudly. He fell asleep and I had to carry him in this precarious position for two hours down a steep mountain trail.

We stopped back in Durango for dinner where you can still get pizza at a sit down restaurant, before driving out to our campsite.

When we arrived, it was drizzling rain, so we got inside the tent and snuggled in our sleeping bags.

At exactly 11:30 pm, I was awakened by a strange smell. It was really bad. Being a father, I am very familiar with bad smells, but this was something entirely new. My first reaction was to open Christian's sleeping bag and hesitantly bend down to take a whiff. I was sure our diet had come back to haunt me. It wasn't Christian. Suddenly the smell seemed to take on a life of its own.

There were two very separate and distinct smells. One was of raw sewage and the other, decomposing flesh. Within a few seconds, I could hear the sounds of some animal rummaging around near the tent. It came to the end of the tent near my head and stuck its nose under the rain fly. It grunted and snorted as it quickly inhaled and exhaled, breathing the smells of my young son and I. The mouth of the bear was less than five inches from my head. The only thing separating it from us was a thin layer of nylon fabric.

Within less than a second, I was enveloped in a cold sweat. Every nerve in my body was alive. I immediately scanned the tent looking for something to use as a weapon. I quickly grabbed for a knife and opened the blade. The likelihood that I would hurt my son or myself if the bear were to aggressively attack seemed too great and I just as quickly replaced the blade.

Over the next 20 minutes, the bear paced back and forth, occasionally snorting and grunting. All the while, I remained completely still and silent, trying to envision all the possible scenarios of attack and how I could protect Christian. My beautiful son lay sleeping, unaware of the potential harm.

The bear abruptly stopped pacing and promptly wandered off. I lay there, drenched in perspiration and prayed.

I figured that the bear was gone for the night. I lay there for over an hour trying to calm down. As I reflected on the event it struck me that animals can literally smell fear. Previously, I only thought of it as a figurative type of cliché. I had experienced my body generate an immediate overload of chemicals and excrete them from every pour. It seemed apparent to me that the bear probably smelled those excretions and became excited.

As I lay there contemplating, the bear returned. I could smell it faintly at first and readily knew it was coming. The smell quickly grew in intensity. I covered both Christian and I in our sleeping bags, hoping to cover any smells we were emitting.

The bear seemed to be more agitated in its pacing. It walked closer to the tent and dislodged the tent stakes. I could hear the ping as they pulled free of the ground. I had tried to move one of the tent stakes earlier, in order to draw the rain fly tauter and could not budge it. This was one powerful animal.

It was taking all of my mental capacity to fight the panic. All of a sudden Christian sat up in his sleeping bag. My new fear was that he would scream and that, in turn, would trigger the bear to attack. He was sound asleep, just sitting there. I tried to push him down. I needed Christian lying flat so that I could perch myself over him and wrap my body around him if the bear did attack. Within a few seconds, Christian relaxed and lay back down. He repeated this three times during the next 15 minutes. It was as if he unconsciously sensed trouble and was trying to react.

Suddenly, the bear stopped pacing. I could feel its body heat as it moved to the side of the tent. It then began to pee alongside and on the tent. When it finished, the bear walked completely around the tent and wandered off again.

At this point, my first reaction was to gather Christian in my arms and run for the car. It then struck me that the bear could be in the area, just far enough away that I could not hear it. If I tried to escape to safety, the bear would give chase and there was no way that I could run faster than a bear, while carrying a 45-pound sleeping child. With much trepidation, I decided to wait out the night. It was now about 2:00 am.

I have never been more awake in my life. There were gallons of adrenaline pumping through my veins. My heart was beating so loudly I could hear it over the light rain beating against the tent. My pulse was so fast that I was afraid of having a heart attack. How could I protect Christian if I was dead from the fright? The rain obscured the sounds outside the tent. I wanted to try and take a peek outside, but couldn't bring myself to unzip the tent and risk alerting the bear.

About another hour had passed. As I lay there, I could only wonder whether that was the end of it. The smell returned.

With this visit, I resigned myself to the facts. The repeated visits from the bear were becoming more hostile. My only concern was about how would the bear attack and could I save Christian.

There was a loud boom, like the sound of a car door slamming. It was startling to both the bear and I. The bear was so close to the tent that when it startled, it leaned into the tent causing the tent to bow in. The bear, with only two thin sheets of tent fabric between us, had firmly pressed against my body. The bear felt hot, and I could feel clumps of matted fur and its large firm muscles. Within an instant it was gone.

Abject terror is the only description that I can provide. I lay there, over my son, no discernable thoughts, only terror. Within a few moments, I saw a flashlight approach the tent. It came right up to the tent and shined onto us. My reaction was to brace myself over Christian. It didn't register in my brain that someone, a person, had come to our aid.

They didn't say anything at all. I couldn't react, my body was driven by pure instinct to protect my son. Who was this person with the flashlight? Why aren't they saying anything? My chance to find out what was happening outside the tent quickly passed. I felt this might have been a fatal mistake.

I was now committed to staying inside the tent and waiting through the night. This was the longest night of my life. At first light, I slowly unzipped the tent, taking at least 10 minutes so as not to make any noise. I unzipped the rain fly with equal caution. After carefully looking around the area, I reassured myself that the bear had gone.

Christian woke as soon as he sensed that I was not beside him. We quickly dressed and I put him in the car as I took the tent down and loaded up. Within 15 minutes, the car was packed and we were driving off the mountain. Within a half hour, we stopped in Durango for food and gasoline. By noon we were back in Albuquerque and met up with Carrie.

While she obviously knew there was a problem from my demeanor and the fact that I looked like heck, I couldn't bring myself to recount the story until later that evening. After telling Carrie, I telephoned the Sheriff's department in Durango. After telling my story to them, they referred me to the park ranger's office. I left repeated messages for the park ranger over the next few days and never received a return call. While I don't know who the person was that probably saved Christian and I from a bear that was becoming increasingly aggressive toward us, I am grateful.

It is now many months since those events and we are planning our next big camping adventure, sans the bear. While

Christian really never consciously knew what happened, he understands that something went on that night.

Everything is back to normal, but the subject of poop still comes up too often.

The Tortoise and the Hare

Mountaineers are an odd bunch of folks who delight in subjecting themselves to all sorts of depraved behaviors. After all, who in their right mind would willingly slog through waist deep snow, travel crevasse filled glaciers, and shinny up vertical rock faces to reach the top of a mountain?

Once up there the only thing to see is where you've been. Although, climb a high enough mountain and you get a glimpse at seeing the curvature of the earth. A ride in an airplane would be much more affordable, including a stay in some posh, sunny, tropical, resort where they put little umbrellas in your drink.

What's more, mountaineers wear the same clothes for weeks at a time, don't take showers, and eat food that is not considered edible by many.

Quite possibly, mountaineers are the genetic mutations of hillbillies from the Deep South. All that's missing is some wicked banjo playing.

Think *Deliverance*.

While anyone who's climbed with me may disagree, confirming their position in the evolutionary ladder, I may be the only exception.

Since I do not have a regular climbing partner I've resorted to renting them on occasion. The bad thing about rentals is that as soon as you figure out how they work you have to return them. The other problem with rentals is that their instructions have long since been lost or discarded and you have to figure them out all on your own.

Each time I set out on a climbing adventure, I set goals for learning specific skills. With any luck, the guide is willing to impart his wisdom and knowledge without being overly critical or making me pick up my toys and go home.

One July in the not too distant past, I convinced my wife that we needed to vacation in Durango Colorado.

It didn't take too much convincing since my wife and I had been traveling to Durango, Colorado for holidays shortly after marrying. Both of us are from small towns nestled in the mountains and being in Durango brought back those good feelings, without having to suffer through an endless visit with relatives.

I found a guiding company run out of Durango and signed up with one of the guides for a two-day trip into the backcountry to climb two peaks - Mt. Snowden, 13,077 feet, and North Twilight Peak, 13,075 feet.

The first morning, I met Bob, the guide, before sunrise and drove 30 miles north, gaining over 5,000 feet in elevation. Bob is a wiry young guy in his twenties. He was so quiet and soft-spoken that I thought he was a deaf mute. At first.

The day began as sunny and cloudless. It looked as if we would escape the smoke of a large wildfire burning out of control in a neighboring valley.

On arriving at the trailhead we made final preparations, packing the food in our backpacks, before hiking for three hours to the base of Mt. Snowden. The climb was mainly 5.5 class rock, consisting of large gray and black blocks, precariously arranged, and growing green with moss. Over the millennia, the weather had broken this mountain into a large pile of rubble, as evidenced by the summit, which was a large dome of loose rock.

After lunching on the summit, we descended on a trail leading from the backside and spiraling down the mountain.

On reaching our gear stash, we loaded up and began a four and a half mile hike to the base of North Twilight peak.

It was about 3:00 pm by the time we started off and my pace steadily slowed. Bob, being in somewhat better shape than I, would dart ahead. The next time I would see him, he would be sitting in the shade of a tree, with his feet up on a rock, sipping water. I would keep on hiking past him and within a few minutes Bob would shoot on by me once more. In the few moments we were near each other, Bob would fire off questions.

"How old are you?"
"How much do you earn?"
"What kind of stocks do you invest in?"
"What does your wife look like?"
"What kind of car do you drive?"

As the day progressed, the heat of the sun and Bob's intermittent barrage of questions became almost unbearable. Smoke poured into the valley, rising steadily into the mountains. My lungs were so saturated and breathing so labored that I lost my voice.

I was almost thankful.

As I plodded along, I was reminded of the story about the turtle and the hare. In this story the two had entered into a relationship whereby the rabbit was going to guide the turtle through the valley, up and down the mountains until they both returned safely home.

Previously the rabbit had, supposedly, guided other turtles through the valley, up and down the mountains until safely returning home. However, the rabbit, confident in his speed, was an arrogant little bag of fur who was not the least bit concerned about the poor turtle whose feet were in agony by this time. At least one little piggy was not a happy camper and was begging for mercy.

The turtle's beak-like nose was a little out of joint since he was paying the rabbit to guide him through the valley and teach him how to "be" a rabbit.

The rabbit was indifferent to the turtle.

This made the turtle mad.

The night was fitful, being cold smoked like a trout or lox, without the bagel.

The turtle and hare set out once again before sunrise. The turtle, painfully sore from trying to keep up with the rabbits pace, was bound and determined to beat him, if not then beat him up. The two raced up the final mountain, North Twilight, reaching the peak well before noon.

The turtle was hiking like his feet were on fire, which was very near true.

The two then practically sprinted the six miles around the mountains and down to the valley floor to the trailhead. The rabbit in fast pursuit.

Sometimes, the best thing about rentals is that you get to return them.

In just over 6 months a new toenail grew back. It has been my experience that the big toe is the one that cried wee-wee-wee all the way home.

Mt. Fuller:
A hunk of cheese, some crackers, and a candy bar

Having so much fun on my prior mountaineering experience in southwestern Colorado, I decided to give it another try. It's like when a food critic tries out a new restaurant, they go back a second time to make sure their first wasn't a fluke.

I contacted the guiding company and arranged a climb of Mt. Fuller, 13,761 feet, and U.S Grant, 13,767 feet, in the San Juan National Forest, about 45 miles north of Durango. The guide, Kevin, spends most of his time in South America guiding climbers on the continent's highest peaks.

We met well before sunrise at their tiny office in an old metal Quonset hut and set off towards Silverton. After driving for about an hour and a half, we turned left off the main road onto a dirt road that led us to a campground that is also the trailhead.

The sun was trying to peek through the dense cloud cover.

The micro weather pattern for this area was predictable, with heavy thunderstorms hitting just after noon every day. This meant that we had to reach our campsite and have it set up before the rain.

I am told that the area is quite beautiful. With all the rainfall, the white, yellow, red and purple wildflowers were in full bloom. The deep green grass was almost waist high. I don't recall seeing much of the colorful foliage. Being paranoid of snakes, I kept my eyes glued to the narrow trail and my ears straining for any telltale rattling.

After several miles of climbing at a steep incline we reached a small lake, touched on one side by a group of mountains. We were a few thousand feet above treeline and the area was like an enormous meadow, with short well-manicured grass. There were marmots living under some large granite rocks nearby, we heard them chirping to one another as we passed. As we set about making camp, they sneaked over to our backpacks, peeking inside for any tasty treats. By this time, the clouds, hanging heavily over the mountains and hiding their summits, turned black. We hurriedly finished just as the clouds opened up, dumping a torrent of water down upon us. There were lightening strikes off in the distance, trailed by loud thundering booms.

In mountaineering, almost all the dangerous climbing takes place in the early morning hours. Getting off the glaciers before the snowbridges over the crevasses weaken. Postholing up to your waist in soft snow isn't much fun either and zaps the energy right out of you. Trying to beat the thunderstorms was an entirely new experience for me though.

After a few hours, the veil lifted, the clouds disappeared and the sun shone brightly. The temperature climbed from 50 to 80 degrees in a matter of minutes. It was like stepping into a sauna.

For the rest of the afternoon I sat patiently waiting for the next big event, dinnertime.

Mountaineering is a sport that involves painfully strenuous activity over untold hours, followed by a nap, and then boredom. Even though I know, when I'm packing for a trip, that I'm going to regularly be bored out of my mind, I consciously leave behind anything of entertainment value. I rationalize that the boredom won't be so bad on this trip. The fact of the matter is that entertainment has weight and weight is heavy, especially after hiking steep mountain trails all day long. Heck, I've even taken to counting the squares of toilet tissue that I'll need for a trip to avoid the extra weight.

After a delectable meal of Chinese noodles, a hunk of cheese, some crackers, and a candy bar, I patiently waited for bedtime.

The next morning we awoke at 4:00 am and readied for the climb up Mt. Fuller. Even though it was August, it was cold. We quickly ate a breakfast of Chinese noodles, a hunk of cheese, some crackers and a candy bar. It didn't seem quite as good as the smorgasbord we'd had for dinner.

We talked little and walked quietly by the light of our headlamps, the only sound coming from the crinkling of our jackets or the swishing of grass against our boots. The high elevation meant that grass and the occasional flower steadily shortened until the plants finally quit growing altogether.

By sunrise we were about 1,000 feet below the summit. We just had to climb a 60 degree snowfield for 500 vertical feet comprised of steadily softening snow, a 350 vertical foot scree field, comprised of small loose rock, and then an easy scramble to the top.

We traversed back and forth across the snowfield, slowly making our way to the scree field. Once there it was so unstable that for every step we seemed to slide down several feet. It was like trying to climb up a waterslide while covered in oil, not that I've ever attempted such a feat.

After struggling a few hours, sliding, falling, cussing and cursing, we reached solid ground and made our way to the summit.

It was approaching noon and the sky was just starting to fill up with fluffy white clouds. We sat down to have lunch - a hunk of cheese, some crackers, and a candy bar. Perhaps we needed less variety.

Within a few minutes of reaching the summit, the clouds blackened and began to lower around us. I was holding my ice axe, made of metal, across my lap, and it began to hum. I flung it off my lap, grabbed my backpack, shoved my food and water bottle inside, and stood up hefting it onto my back. As I reached for my ice axe I looked up to see Kevin doing the same.

The base of the black storm clouds was mere feet above our heads.

Without saying a word we quickly began our descent. Coming off the solid ground onto the scree, I took big steps, letting the natural rock slides hasten my way. By the time we reached the snowfield I was trotting straight down hill, stopping only when one of my legs would sink waist deep into the snow, giving me pause to turn and look up the mountain to see that the summit was now hidden from view in the black clouds.

Within 15 to 20 minutes we had descended the 1,000 vertical feet and were hotfooting our way to camp, about a mile away and 2,000 vertical feet below.

In this very short time, day had turned to night.

Rain began to fall, tiny droplets at first and then increasing in both size and velocity.

We reached camp just as the rain turned to hail. I glanced at my temperature gauge, it was 78 degrees. We climbed into the tent to wait out the storm. Within 30 minutes the temperature had dropped to 25 degrees. Since I wasn't prepared for such cold weather, I draped my sleeping bag over my shoulders to try and get warm. Lightening was striking simultaneously with the deafening sound of thunder all around our tent. We folded our sleeping pads and sat on our heels on top of them in the event we were struck by the lightening.

At first it was terrifying. As the hours passed it became tedious. Eventually I got to the point where I thought, "If the lightening is going to strike us, get it over with already." My legs had long since cramped and my feet were numb.

A hunk of cheese, some crackers, and a candy bar

My newfound ambivalence must have done something, because we could hear the thunder ebb away from us and then the hail stopped abruptly. I poked my head out of the tent to see the ground covered in hail measuring a foot deep. Just as suddenly as the sky darkened, the sun came out. I moved outside, still wrapped in my sleeping bag, making my way over to a large rock to sit upon. Waiting for dinnertime to roll around, and having no other entertainment, I watched my temperature gauge rise, as if it had been moved from the freezer to a hot oven. Within minutes we were back in the sauna. Within half an hour all the hail had melted and the ground was dry in another hour.

The next morning we again awoke early, and choked down a hearty breakfast of Chinese noodles, a hunk of cheese, some crackers, and a candy bar. By sunrise the weather clouds were already forming so we decided to abort climbing another peak and hurry down the mountain.

Initially, my thoughts were to hurry so as to avoid the thunderstorm. As we passed below treeline I began to have visions of hamburgers and french fries that kept me moving at a pretty good pace.

Experienced mountaineers often recommend that you take along your favorite foods because at high altitude, eating anything is difficult and you stand a better chance with your favorite foods. I think it really doesn't matter because if you eat your favorite foods often enough, when you aren't even hungry, they quickly become your least favorite foods.

Although, Chinese noodles, a hunk of cheese, some crackers, and a candy bar sound pretty good right now.

Mt Fay: Married With Children

My family's vacations are always somewhat spontaneous even though we always seem to migrate to the same place, namely the Banff – Lake Louise area, two or three times each year.

I had only been planning my semi-annual mountaineering trip for a couple of weeks and was finding it difficult to get things scheduled in such a short timeframe. While I have been climbing for several years now, I don't know anyone, who I would trust with my life, who climbs. So I'll usually "partner" with a local mountaineering guide. While "partner" serves my delusions of adequacy, the reality is that we both take a risk on the unknown, theirs somewhat higher than mine.

I benefit by knowing that in Canada a certified guide has a known base level of practical experience and knowledge. The guide, on the other hand, is dealing with someone that has less ability than their own and therefore bears responsibility for decisions. July and August are peak months for climbers coming into the area and none of the guides I know were available.

Generally, I'll go up and climb for several days and then my wife and son join me for a family vacation. I had pretty much given up on climbing this year and was beginning to resolve myself to a few solo climbs, a reckless pursuit indeed.

On the day prior to leaving work for vacation, I did a quick Internet search and found a new guiding agency. In a half-hearted attempt, I left a voicemail message and within a few minutes had a return call and was able to lock in a climb. My plan was to climb Mt. Victoria and Mt. Lefroy. Anyone who has ever seen a photograph of Lake Louise will notice these glacier and snow covered peaks at the far end of the lake.

My partner for the climb was going to be Sylvia, a certified guide and warden for the Jasper National Park. She had, literally, just returned from climbing in Bolivia and Ecuador while on holiday. After learning of her impressive mountaineering exploits, I was expecting this tall, broad, former East German concentration camp guard with a full beard.

That night I packed my climbing gear. The next morning, I awoke early and began re-packing. My now eight-year-old son, Christian, heard me shuffling around and came to help. We sat at the top of the second floor staircase talking about his week and plans for our upcoming vacation. As usually happens, our he-man testosterone kicked in and we began wrestling. Usually, this is where he hurts me and I have to tell Mom on him. Today though, I had the brilliant idea of teaching my son the art of stair surfing. You know, sliding on your stomach headfirst down the stairs. I remembered doing this when I was around his age. I blame the eventuality on my son, for if I had known he was already an expert stair surfer, I would not have tried so hard to beat him. You see, in our semi-final match-up, I was trailing by a wisp when I heard this loud POP. In all honesty, I'm not sure whether I first heard it or felt it. Christian has tried to counsel me on the physics of what happened, but I still get a little nauseous.

It was my rib that popped - one of those little jobbers on the bottom of the rack. I have broken many bones in my day, all in the name of extracurricular activity. My rib cage is now comprised of healed fractures. There is no longer any undamaged bone left. Historically, I had been involved in some kind of sport and didn't really notice when the bones would break, so this was a new experience for me. My wife mustered enough sympathy to point out that old people who don't take care of themselves get brittle with age. She offered me a glass of calcium fortified milk. Such loving advice and concern.

I was set to fly out of Dallas for Calgary that afternoon for three days of fairly strenuous climbing. And I had a newly broken rib. The realization was that the trip was already paid for and besides, I would rest easy on the flight to Calgary and by the next morning it would be fine. I met Sylvia at Moraine Lake at 10:00 am, a full hour past our scheduled time, but she was not at all perturbed – try that one in the U.S. Sylvia wasn't at all what I expected.

I had a lot of explaining to do when I got home.

It turns out that Sylvia is a backcountry warden and alpine specialist involved with rescue and training other park wardens. As a mountaineer, Sylvia has climbed all over the world and actually summitted Denali, the highest mountain in North America, at the age of 23.

My wife was going to kill me.

My goals were quite simple: experience some classic Canadian mountaineering; develop my glacier and route-finding skills; and not die in the process. Not necessarily in that order.

Due to the unseasonably warm weather, the snow on Mt. Victoria and Mt. Lefroy was out of shape. Recent climbers in the area reported that they were post-holing to their hip in the soft snow. As is often the case, a "Plan B" was needed. After some discussion, and quick maneuvering to get the hut permits rearranged, we decided upon climbing Mt. Fay in the Valley of Ten Peaks as the primary objective.

We left from Moraine Lake, which is several miles into the mountains behind Lake Louise in the heart of the Canadian Rockies. We took the Parren route up to the Neil Colgan hut, the highest point of permanent habitation in Canada. Less than 12 hours earlier I had been in Dallas, at 550 feet above sea level. From the Moraine Lake Lodge we would climb 3,600 vertical feet in less than five kilometers. It would take seven hours to reach the Neil Colgan hut, our base of operation.

The approach route took us up some fifth class, vertical, rock cliffs. This route kept us from spending too much time climbing or crossing the exposed paths of tremendous hanging seracs that crowned the route. Occasionally, we would hear the resounding boom and feel the winds brought on by a piece of the glacier breaking free and crashing down the gullies.

The high winds blew glacial melt-water right back up the rock face. The temperature of the water was probably somewhere around 35 degrees Fahrenheit. Talk about an exhilarating shower. The good news is that the intensity of the winds only picked up when we were near any cascading water. What luck.

When we arrived we had the hut all to ourselves. High above Moraine Lake and the tree line, the Neil Colgan hut is a fine place to view how the changing weather serves to create a wonderful and constantly changing experience. Although the gale force winds at the hut, bite.

This hut was named after a warden, Neil Colgan, who was patrolling the backcountry on horseback in 1979, and was killed when his horse kicked him in the chest. It wasn't instantaneous though and as he lay dying he wrote a letter to his family and friends. A terrible thought but the views from the hut make it certainly understandable why someone would take up a risky career that would allow them to realize this experience.

The next morning we arose at 4:00 am and were dressed, fed, and enroute via the Central Ice Bulge Direct by 5:30 am. Here I might add that after a strenuous work out, the affects of altitude worked wonders for my broken rib. Even after taking a sleeping pill, I had to sleep twisted up like a corkscrew. When I awoke the pain from my rib was greatly diminished – probably because the rest of my body was so cramped and sore. No wonder modern chiropractic medicine thrives.

The sun was just coming over the horizon, and the distant mountains were silhouetted by the yellow-orange hues of the rising sun against a backdrop of deep blue sky. We were roped together, with a good 30 meters between us. The low temperatures at night created a nice, thick, frozen crust on the glacier. It took a good 60 minutes of glacial travel around Mt. Little. Looking back at our tracks, I could hardly see the crampon marks. At the base of Mount Fay there was a bergschrund – a crevasse where the glacier pulls away from the side of a mountain - that proved easily crossed, due in large part to the early season conditions and good snow pack. From the bergschrund to the ridgeline the angle was about 300 vertical feet at a 50+ degree angle that required us to kick steps in the hard crusted snow and to climb sections of ice by kicking the front-point of our crampons into the ice.

Once on the ridgeline each pitch was uneventful and each section was straightforward with good solid belay sites. Every now and then when I would glance downward, there were moments of vertigo but I was just too busy to dwell on it. Even though the limestone is quite weathered and rotten in many places, we climbed carefully, neither causing nor seeing much in the way of rock fall. Climbing along the ridge gave us wonderful views to the Moraine Lake Valley and the Larch Valleys. The mountain, with its arêtes and gendarme, gave us some good 5.6 class rock, meaning vertical rock face with good handholds.

I must admit that it was a first, when Sylvia accused me of being nimble. I put the comment into proper perspective and was sure that she was just grateful that I hadn't set off any major rockslides.

To reach the summit, we crossed a large snowfield. The summit of Mt. Fay, at 10,600 feet, was crowned with a large snow cornice hanging at least 15 to 20 feet out over the valley with over 1,000 foot vertical drop below.

It had taken us three and a half hours to reach the summit from the Colgan hut. After a leisurely lunch of pepperoni sausage, hunk of cheddar cheese and a candy bar, we began the descent. There was nothing but blue sky, not a cloud to be seen. The wind was quite chilly but it was hot with the sun beating down on us. It was like putting one foot on a block of ice and the other on hot coals – so on average it was just right.

The snow we had ascended had softened as a result of the hot sun and the angle of the slopes. Coming down off the ridgeline and onto the glacier the angle was too steep to glissade, so we reppelled, fixing new repel anchors along where the glacier touched tall vertical rock faces. The snow had softened to the point that I was post-holing up to my thighs. Sylvia, being somewhat lighter than I, seemed to have no problems.

The trek back to the Colgan hut was easy going, with only a few spots where we would post-hole to our waist. This can be quite deceptive, given that it is still a massive, living, unyielding glacier over 1,200 feet thick. Glacier travel can be somewhat unnerving in those instances when one leg would post-hole to my waist and my foot would swing freely. Standing on a failing snow-bridge over a crevasse has the effect of instantaneously increasing the ole' adrenaline flow and jolting one into action on the double-quick.

Upon arriving back at the Neil Colgan hut, we napped and relaxed for a few hours before climbing Mt. Bowlen (3,071 meters) before dinner. While very intimidating from Moraine Lake, the summit of Mt. Bowlen is a fourth class, steep but not vertical, scramble from the hut, with an elevation gain of 500 feet. It takes 20 to 30 minutes from the hut to the summit. Not bad for a major peak in the Canadian Rockies, and speaks to the effort already undertaken to reach elevation at the hut.

This is easily one of the most satisfying mountaineering experiences I've had - a challenging objective, great climbing companion and the splendor of the Canadian Rockies. Adapting to life back in corporate America would be a tough transition.

It turned out that my biggest challenge was explaining to my wife about climbing with a strong, attractive woman with whom I have quite a bit in common. Alas, I am but a stupid man. Reliving the trip for my wife, I may have mentioned Sylvia's name once too often. It wasn't until a few weeks after the trip when my wife happened to place a sharp well-aimed shot, catching me off guard and right between the eyes.

"I really wish you wouldn't keep talking about her."

My attempts at humor to improve her mood didn't help. Carrie's glare cut me to the quick.

I got the hint.

Oh well, she'll get over it. Although, I probably should have waited before announcing that I was hoping to climb Huayna Potosi in Bolivia and wondered aloud whether Sylvia would be available.

Ice Climbing

The Canadian Rockies are well known throughout the world for its many mountaineering opportunities. Its ice climbs are especially sought after objectives due to the variations, complexity, height and the surrounding wilderness.

The thing that attracted me to ice climbing is one of the most simplistic differences it has from rock climbing. In rock climbing you're stuck using whatever hand and foot holds that God has chosen when she built the mountains. God has a wonderful sense of humor. By contrast, in ice climbing you get to choose, more-or-less, where to place the ice axe to create the hand holds and the crampon points for foot holds.

I have absolutely no recollection as to why I even chose to undertake a six-day waterfall ice-climbing course in the Canadian Rockies. My vague recollection has something to do with developing skills to become a more well-rounded and competent mountaineer. However, I am pretty round as it is, and as for competency – yeah, right.

The certified guides who would be our instructors for the week were Mike and Grant. They assigned us the label of "Hodad" (Hō-Dad). Although they refused to tell us exactly what a Hodad is, it apparently is some kind of climbing novice.

My wife refers to this as being a "Gumby," which she defines as a neophyte, not too bright who cheerfully takes all manners of abuse and punishment, such as having body parts physically wrenched in all possible manners.

I really hoped that wasn't the definition of a Hodad.

There were seven of us taking the course, four from Canada and three from the United States. Dan is a diver in the Canadian Navy - I didn't know that Canada even had a Navy. Keith works in the oil patch selling devices that steam liquefies the oil for extraction. Mike Butler is a ski patroller and rigger for movies. The lone woman was a dentist who only works three days a week and to whom I gave unending grief for being so privileged.

The U.S. contingent consisted of myself and two guys from San Francisco. I know what you're thinking and you're only half right. Franz and Mike, whom I referred to as Hans and Franz. You can never have too many guys named Mike in the same group. Although when you call out, "Hey Mike," the odds are pretty good that someone will respond.

During the week our group climbed challenging objectives at some of the most beautiful places in the world such as Johnston Canyon, Kings Creek and Haffner Creek. There were a few days in which additional guides were brought in and we divided up by skill level into groups of two. Even though I didn't have any apparent skill, I was allowed to climb. On those days the objectives were multi-pitch routes, most notably Lake Louise Falls and Cascade Falls.

Each day we met for coffee and were on the road before 8:00 am. We usually hiked into the days climbing objective in time to see the sun coming up over the mountains. There was always at least six inches of fresh powder on the ground to trudge through and the temperature hovered between cold and colder (+15F to -5F) without taking into account wind chill or the fact that we were perched on a frozen hunk of ice.

The second day of the course we drove to Peter Lougheed Provincial Park to climb a waterfall in the Kings Creek area. The hike from the car was about 30 minutes. The morning started off bitterly cold and seemed to have no plans for changing as the day progressed. Having been wearing shorts in Dallas just three days prior, I was still acclimating to the temperature and was wearing about five or six layers of fleece and Gore-Tex. Generally speaking, when moving, you warm up, and when standing still, you get cold. So it only goes to say that if you are planning to move you should get ready by making sure you have the appropriate layering and same goes if you are going to be standing still. Needless to say, within several minutes of leaving the car, I was stopping to remove some of the layers. I dressed and undressed more times this one day than I had the entire year.

By the end of the day when it was time to hike back to the car I still hadn't learned my lesson. Within sight of the car I stopped to remove my heavy gloves because they were full of sweat. I stashed them in my backpack and started hiking again. In just a few minutes my sweaty hands were ice cold so I shoved them in my jacket pockets.

As a kid, my father used to get so mad at me when I would walk around with my hands in my pockets. If he said it once he said it two million times, "One of these days you're going to trip and fall and break your neck, and when you do, don't come crying to me." I never took his advice and would regularly stick my hands in my pockets whenever I got the opportunity. After all, if God didn't want me putting my hands in my pockets why did she give us pockets? Even though I lived on the edge, walking around with my hands in my pocket, I somehow managed to reach my current age, 30 and some, with a great deal of luck. Not to mention good balance.

As I marched through the snow, with the car parked just at the top of hill in front of me, I kicked a stone. It must have been a pretty good-sized boulder because when my foot hit my whole leg vibrated. In one smooth six-million-dollar-man kind of second I went crashing to the ground like an old log. Twisting and writhing as I went to avoid smacking my face on the ground, I landed on my left side. Since I was the first one coming out and knowing there were eight people behind me, the embarrassment factor kicked-in and I was instantly standing again – neck intact.

I managed to break three ribs in that epic brush with death. They instantly swelled up and popped in-and-out of place for the next several weeks. When I moved just right the pain was sufficient enough that my whole body instantly stiffened and I made a strange "SSSHHUUUH" sound while inhaling. By the end of the course I found that I could no longer reach to close the car door with my left hand and sitting down required several gyrations to get my hips and back aligned just right, almost like a woman nine months pregnant.

While climbing at Johnston Canyon, I became the poster child for bad technique. Holding an ice axe as delicately as you are supposed to hold a golf club, tennis racket, or polo mallet sounds easy enough. I know it sounds strange but there is something different about trying to gently hold an ice axe while it is supporting you 30 feet off the ground. My body subconsciously worked to offset the fact that only a few millimeters of the ice axe pick was imbedded in the ice. I held the handles of the axe with a death grip heretofore unknown by any human. By the end of that one day, my forearms grew to exceed even Popeye's. I later learned that it was really lactic acid that had built up when parts of my forearms actually began to dissolve and burn away. Or so it felt.

My climbing partner, Butler, was belaying me. I tried to give up several times but he refused to lower me down until I had completed the climb. With Butler's "encouragement" I managed to struggle to the top and had learned my lesson and no longer held a death grip on the axes. Even though I had lost the feeling in my hands Butler still had a difficult time prying my fingers from his throat.

Important mental and physical health tip: Never make jokes about your climbing partner until you no longer depend on him for your life or to let you down from something really high off the ground.

While staying at a hostel in Banff, I was talking to some young women from Australia one morning while preparing my peanut butter sandwich's for breakfast and lunch (eating diverse foods is essential to maintaining strength). Almost in unison the two women asked me why I climbed mountains and frozen waterfalls.

Not to say that this was the first time I was asked that question. My wife asks all the time. The tone of her voice or timing of her question always seems to make me a bit defensive though. But, these Australian girls seemed genuinely interested and caught me completely off guard. It made me pause and actually think about it for a moment as I had put off ever thinking about it long enough. I supposed it was my way of being an explorer, a pioneering spirit, of dealing with my fears and feeling alive. I explained that when I am on a shear wall of ice, held on by only a few millimeters of steel, my mind is instantly cleared of all trivial matters. As a matter of fact, I regularly forget to even blink or breathe as I cling to the side of a frozen waterfall. Not that I was all that excited about breathing after surviving my epic encounter with the rock buried under the snow.

The world is instantly transformed into a simplistic survival mode. All the people I offended at the office, while driving my car, at the restaurant, or just plain stupid people, seem insignificant. Knowing that they're probably all rooting for me to fall makes me want to survive out of spite.

One morning, within minutes of starting to climb Cascade Falls, a grade-three waterfall, three of us who were roped together broke equipment. The temperature was bitterly cold, -15°F and the ice very hard. Mike, the guide, and I both broke a pick on our ice axes while Butler broke a crampon point.

As soon as we completed that pitch the guide quickly brought out a repair kit and changed his pick.

He looked over at me said, "Sorry. Tough break. I don't have any other spares so you'll just have to struggle with that one."

Knowing what lay in store for me as I looked at the remaining route up frozen waterfall I was reminded of another tragic event in my life.

When I was five-years-old, my brother, sisters and I were at my grandparent's house. Our grandfather had given us each enough money to buy an ice cream cone. It was mid-August and really hot outside. We kids all walked down to the Dairy Queen and I bought a nice chocolate dipped cone. We rarely had this kind of opportunity so this was really a treat. I was so excited. As we started back to our grandparent's house I had barely eaten much of the plasticized chocolate flavored crust when I tripped and dropped my cone. By the way, neither hand was in a pocket. Panic and despair coursed through every vein in my body. At five years old it was all I could do to fight back the tears and sobbing. I finally lost it there on the sidewalk, my brother, sisters, and I standing around my poor fallen dessert treat.

I stood silently looking from the guide to my ice axe with a forlorn expression on my face. The same emotions of that five-year-old child holding an empty and broken ice cream cone tugged on my heartstrings as I looked up at the remaining six pitches, or rope lengths, of the climb. It was all I could do to hold back the sobbing.

About two inches of my right ice axe pick had broken cleanly away as I pulled the axe from the frozen waterfall to strike a new placement. Further inspection of the break revealed rust that meant the pick had been partially fractured for some time. In other words it wasn't my fault. This is important since the axe was a rental. If I had my precious multi-tool knife thingy, which I unceremoniously ejected from my backpack that morning due to it's excessive weight, I would have been able to file down the pick into something resembling a blade. Of course, it probably would have taken me a week, with the amount of metal I had to file.

The rest of the day turned out to be quite fun as I repeatedly beat that broken axe into the ice in the faint hope of getting a good purchase so as not to plummet to my death. Albeit my definition of fun had to be drastically revised in a sort of sadomasochistic kind of way.

While we climbed, I alternated cursing the axe with prayers for my life – I was taking no chances. Placing that ice axe was like pounding the ice with a large hammer. Ice constantly broke apart flying in all directions. Large pieces would careen down the mountain much to the dismay of my comrade, Butler, who was below me.

Important mental and physical health tip: Never make jokes about your climbing instructor until you no longer depend on him for your life or to lend you spare equipment when you're really high off the ground.

The one factor that made this course so successful was the people. Whenever a group of relative strangers gets together, acting on our best behavior only lasts so long before true personalities begin to emerge. Without the sense of humor and adaptability of my fellow climbers and the guides, we could not have learned all that we did or reach the level of climbing skill in such a short time.

An event like this is something that I try to adapt into my personal life. Whether it is at home or work. I try not to take myself too seriously because I hope no one else does. A sense of humor sure helps to keep things in proper perspective, especially when I'm dangling a few hundred feet off the ground, grasping the frozen skin of a waterfall with a few millimeters of steel.

Avalanche

Growing up in a large family meant money was scarce during my youth. It didn't help that Montana had the lowest per capita income in the United States. If I wanted to enjoy luxuries, I had to be industrious. One time I traded some well-read comic books for a big, old, multi-tool knife in order to trade it for an ancient pair of warped skis. When placed side by side they bowed out from one another. I bought a pair of leather ski boots at a garage sale for two dollars. They were so old they could have been made from Wooly Mammoth hide and used in the last ice age.

At every opportunity I hiked up the sleigh hill near our home and attempted to ski down. This consisted of my placing the skis together and pointing them straight downhill. The bend in the skis caused each one to point to a different side of the run. Within a few seconds of launching I would approach the speed of sound, loose control, and crash into one of the many boulders and trees that lined the sleigh hill. As the pain of my bumps and bruises subsided, I dug through the snow to find my skis, boots, odd article of clothing, and try again.

I learned to ski purely from trial and error. And there was a lot of error.

When I was older, and my grandmother passed away, my father divided her savings among all her grandchildren. Instead of saving my share for something practical, I bought brand new skis, boots, poles, and clothing. I had just enough money left over to actually go skiing at a real ski area for the season. I loved to go fast and I loved to race. It would take me about ten minutes to go up the mountain on the chair lift and two minutes to get down. I hadn't yet quite got the knack for turning.

A few years later a friend and I were racing each other down a giant-slalom racecourse. As a result of that tomfoolery I spent most of my senior year of high school in the hospital.

During my sophomore year of college my brother talked me into going skiing again. We ended up going to the Big Sky resort. After several runs on progressively more difficult terrain we went to the top of the mountain. We skied to the edge of a powder filled bowl with our skis hanging over the edge at a perpendicular angle.

We jumped onto the slope and after 3 or 4 turns I fell. I wallowed in the fresh powder up to my chest and spent the next hour looking for one of my skis. I must have looked like a moron out there, wailing away with one ski trying to shovel off the side of the mountain. As soon as I found my ski I was off that run in milliseconds and onto one with hard pack. Those three turns would be my sum total experience with powder skiing.

It wouldn't be until 15 years later that I would try skiing again. This time with my wife and five-year-old son. We've skied a few weeks each year for the past few years. My son, Christian, has acquired a taste for skiing fast and I faithfully follow behind as he speeds down the mountain.

With the indelible memory of a ski accident that resulted in me having two vertebrae in my lower back fused together, and specific instructions never to ski again, it seemed only natural that I would decide to take an avalanche course that would have me backcountry skiing 2,500 vertical feet so I could ski powder while dodging trees, rock outcroppings and other natural hazards, all for the sake of identifying potential avalanche activity.

Having an avalanche certification could come in handy back home in Texas. I secretly hoped that it would give me an edge in becoming the states first official avalanche forecaster.

Just about anything can happen in Texas, after all, George Bush did become president and he can't even speak a coherent sentence.

There were four potential victims for the instructor in the Advanced Avalanche Awareness Course. We had a couple from Ottawa, Beata and Ian, and a schoolteacher, Bonnie, from Whitefish Montana, who would be using the training to teach students about avalanche safety in her Earth Science class. The instructor, Burke Duncan, is a professional avalanche forecaster for Alberta's Kananaskis Country and a certified ski guide. This course would turn out to be one of the most intensive learning experiences I've endured. Excuse me, I mean enjoyed.

The most important thing I learned from Burke during this grueling course was that Canadians are so unsure of themselves. They turn every statement into a question by finishing it with, "Eh?"

It's a beautiful day today! Eh? Even in situations where they are clearly an expert authority:

"We can see there's been some recent avalanche activity on that mountain today! Eh?"

This is compounded by the influence of Australians who flock to the region to enjoy the mountains and work in the service industries.

Australians have a wonderful laidback attitude, "No worries mate!"

The Canadians have adopted this attitude but are just too unsure of themselves - "No worries! Eh?"

I suppose it could be something having to do with some biological phenomenon on the North American continent by which the further one travels northward the level of arrogance and egotism declines. I'm sure some crafty American will discover and market a "cure" for it.

Each day of this six-day course we were ready by 8:00 am and finished the day around 10:00 pm. While each day would begin and end in the classroom we would have a field trip into some of the most beautiful country I've ever seen. Each day began by researching the area we planned to ski. There are two categories of information gathering: 1) free and 2) paid for.

The free information consisted of reviewing published (via the Internet) avalanche forecasts, weather forecasts, satellite weather maps, along with information gleaned from guide books and prior avalanche accident reports. While out in the bush we did ski pole tests to quickly evaluate the layers of the snow – depth, crusts, etc. We did hand tests which consisted of using our hands and ski poles to "carve" out a block of snow all the way to ground level and then using our hands and arms to steadily apply pressure from the uphill side of the block until it broke in order to evaluate snow stability and composition of the weak layers.

The information we paid for was through sweat equity. This consisted of digging pits and performing snow study tests. The granddaddy of the paid-for information was the Rutschblock test that consists of digging a large "U" shaped pit and having a skier stand on top applying more and more pressure until one of the snow layers fails.

We used snow study kits, consisting of a wooden folding ruler, metal card with various sized grids etched into it, a magnifying lens and thermometers to identify and evaluate the different layers within the snow pack and types of snow crystals. Temperature ratings are taken, the type of snow crystals recorded and the hardness of each snow layer recorded. All this information can then be plotted to identify the exact stability of that particular area of snow pack.

Before this course I thought there were two kinds of snow, sticky and non-sticky, with the only reason to care being if you wanted to make snowballs and snowmen. Nonstick snow is somehow related to crunching Styrofoam and the sound of fingernails on a chalkboard.

As it turns out, snow is a fascinating subject. Not only are there different types of snow crystals that fall to the ground, they change as they age, based on temperature, other snow, rain, sun, moisture in the air, pressure, etc. I can't wait for the one day it snows in Dallas each year.

There are four basic points of evaluation we had to continually consider while playing in the snow:

What is the terrain like? Is there any current avalanche activity? What is the grade of the slope? Any slope greater than 30 degrees is prime for avalanches. What is the aspect? Meaning the effect of sun, wind, etc., on the slope.

What are the current snow pack conditions? Are there unstable layers? Where? What is the load on the unstable layers? Adhesion or cohesion of the snow crystals?

What are the risks? Would I be swept over cliffs, rocks, trees? Would I be buried? Are conditions changing? Are conditions getting better or worse as the day progresses?

By evaluating the answers to these questions in concert with one another a picture becomes clear as to what action should be taken. Do I really want to ski / climb / hike here? Is there a safer alternative?

The process of breaking down a potential life-threatening situation into simple questions seemed so logical that the same process could be used in every day life.

During this course, skiing was integral in getting into and out of the avalanche terrain. My mode of transportation was Alpine Touring skis, which are downhill skis with hinged bindings that allowed me to cross country ski. On the descent I would lock the heels into place for downhill skiing. Throughout the course we were in powder that was over five feet deep. Since my previous experience skiing in powder consisted of three turns and an hour of digging for a ski, you can imagine my level of excitement. I loved skiing up the mountain but the descent left something to be desired. One day we skied 2,500 vertical feet in the Bow Summit area. On our descent I quickly ascertained that falling in five feet of powder is like trying to swim with, well, skis on. Falling was like jumping off a diving board. It must have looked like I was trying to perfect as many dives as possible. Eventually Burke gingerly skied over to inform me that the effort to recover from a fall was equivalent to the energy expended on an entire run. I must have made 50 "runs" going down that one mountain.

Another day we skied 1,500 vertical feet along a ring of mountains in the Spray Lakes area to inspect a recent avalanche. It was a cold day and we encountered winds of 100 km/hour by the time we reached the site. The wind whipped the snow into near whiteout conditions. I could have enjoyed it for hours, but no, we had to descend. I locked my heels onto the skis and proceeded to cartwheel, fall and generally ping-pong my way down the mountain through a forest of large pine trees.

Trees are hard.

While I did my best to limit any photos, the opportunities were too great for my wonderful teammates to resist and I'm sure they'll turn up just as I'm being nominated to run for president and ruin the whole thing.

Each day we spent time in mock avalanche rescue situations where we practiced using avalanche transceivers and probes to locate victims. We went through a specific process of questioning any witnesses, assigning roles and responsibilities, and choosing the terrain to search - especially in cases where the victim didn't have a transceiver.

In North America each year there are too many preventable avalanche related deaths. The victims either suffocate or die through trauma (i.e. hitting trees, rocks, etc). Realistically, the time right after an avalanche contains precious few minutes by which to locate a victim and perform the rescue. The challenge for the rescuers is not to give up in spite of the anguish and the sheer amount of effort it takes. There can be air pockets where the victim protected their mouth with their hands or came to rest near a tree or rock that has aided their rescue.

While there are natural triggers such as animals, falling rocks, falling clumps of snow (i.e., from a tree), almost all avalanches affecting humans are triggered by humans. So, it only makes sense that if we go into avalanche terrain we have the knowledge, skills, and tools to survive.

I quickly found that checking the gear of my teammates was a key element of my survival.

Were all of our transceivers working correctly? Did we have shovels and probes stored inside our backpacks?

I often told my teammates that if we were caught in an avalanche that I wanted them to have the best transceivers and be the most well trained in their use to ensure they could find me quickly.

When we talked about victim survivability I put my teammates on notice that if it were me under the snow that they were not allowed to squander my time by leaving to get help. While I may have said these things jokingly, I certainly meant every word. Leaving the scene to get help means body recovery not rescue.

Our last activity of the course was to find four victims of a mock avalanche. Two of the victims used transceivers and two did not. My job was to lead the rescue.

Responsibilities were assigned to each of us. Burke was the dazed but miraculous survivor. Beata and Ian assembled the shovels while Bonnie and I searched using the transceivers. Within minutes we located the victims who used transceivers and quickly dug them out. Beata and Ian searched for clues along the snow pack – gloves, skis, poles anything that might belong to one of the missing climbers. They probed the uphill sides of trees searching for a body that may have gotten hung up, all to no avail.

We then re-grouped and started a probe-line whereby we got in a spaced line and began systematically probing the avalanche path from top down. Time was passing and it was clear that those victims who had not used a transceiver were losing the battle. Luckily, in our case the victims were a backpack and an insulated lunch bag.

The experience instilled enough fear in me to ensure that I will make every effort to play by the rules. Although, my wife and son get embarrassed when I force them to put their transceivers on to go outside and play with the dog.

You just never know.

After all, winter in Dallas just begs for an avalanche.

The day after completing our course, there was an accident less than 100 miles north of where we were that involved three Wardens. They had just completed digging a snow pit as part of their avalanche forecast program and were skiing out of the area. All three were caught and buried in a slab avalanche. One of them was somehow able to extricate himself. He searched the surface and discovered a hand sticking out of the snow. He dug the warden out of the snow and found he was not breathing, had no pulse, and a broken leg. After clearing the airway and giving a couple of breaths he began to breathe. He then turned his attention to the third victim and was able to locate him using an avalanche transceiver but he was buried 5 feet down in the snow. Without help, he dug this warden out of the snow and found that he too was not breathing and had no pulse. CPR was initiated and the victim was flown to the hospital but he didn't survive. All this was done in just 25 minutes. Given the circumstances it's easy to see where all the time went and further indicates just how difficult these situations can become.

As professionals, these wardens are in avalanche terrain every day and their job is to forecast avalanche activity. As people go out into the backcountry it is imperative not only to have the right equipment but to be well practiced in its use. The technology of avalanche transceivers seems to be straightforward and simplistic. However, looking for a victim of an avalanche is no time to learn how to use it.

I found that the value of this avalanche awareness course isn't just for those of us who desire to gain the knowledge to support us in other dangerous pursuits, such as ice climbing, alpine touring, cross-country skiing, mountaineering, etc. Anyone who ventures into the backcountry or skis out-of-bounds at recreational ski areas needs to be well aware of the consequences. In many places the avalanche dangers are year round.

Each of us needs to gain and maintain the skills so that we are prepared in whatever endeavor we set our sights.

If I'm ever a victim of an avalanche, or anything else for that matter, and you are around, I really want you to have good equipment and great skills.

Do unto others, as you would have them to do unto you…

Friendship

Good friends are the people in our lives that refuse to leave despite whatever you do to them. Their friendship transcends time and distance.

This is good because as a man, I'm genetically programmed to not talk on the telephone for more than a few minutes before my body begins to melt. It's kind of like the Wicked Witch of the West when she gets water dumped on her.

Even though I'm absolutely horrible at writing letters, I've improved with the advent of the Internet and electronic mail. Through this wonderful medium, which is often way too slow at delivering or retrieving messages, I've been able to rekindle a few of my old friendships, marred by time and rekindle new friendships marred by distance.

I would like to thank former Vice President Gore for his fight to provide the funding in the Senate for the invention of the Internet. That in itself is an interesting story of how people choose to believe the worst in others. In this case, a noted reporter interviewed Mr. Gore who made a statement about being the most staunch supporter for funding the invention of the Internet. Mr. Gore's Republican "friends" helped him out by restating his comment as if Mr. Gore himself were taking credit for inventing the Internet and then did a bums-rush on the media. Those jokesters really pulled one over because America bought it hook, line, and sinker.

Perhaps President Bush, the sequel, should have a technology summit with Mr. Gore and maybe even the transportation department. In a visit to Concord, New Hampshire Mr. Bush is quoted as asking, "Will the highways on the Internet become more few?"

I merely bring this up as an example of friendship and practical jokes. For the record, let me clarify that I think all politicians are, by definition, as crooked and self-serving as the day is long. Talk about procrastination. At some point in time you and I really need to fix this mess.

Please don't send me any political hate mail though.

I digress. Sometimes it's pretty difficult to differentiate between friend and enemy. Sure, friends are sometimes more cruel than even your worst enemy. Most of the time though this type of friend is a family member.

Growing up in my house, the chores were equally divided with the boys working outside and the girls working inside. There were five kids, two boys and three girls. Looking back on it, my parents probably divided up the chores that way to avoid bloodshed and bitter family divisions. We were not the Brady Bunch and my sisters certainly weren't Marcia, Jan, or Cindy.

My brother, Roy, is four years older than I. While we were growing up we fought tooth and nail. Strangely enough the intensity of our fighting would usually increase whenever we had to do chores together, especially those difficult or boring.

It would go something like this. Mom or Dad would tell us to do something immediately. Over the course of the next few hours they would regularly repeat it, steadily getting louder and more demanding. Eventually my brother and I would get tired of hearing about it and start the work. After a few minutes I would end up doing something to upset Roy, usually something like breathing the wrong way. This would be followed by something else he didn't like me doing. Generally after fifteen minutes or so, I would end up getting yelled at or punched in the arm. Either way, this was my signal to scream in pain and call out to my mom. After pleading my case, Roy would get in trouble and we would commence work. Strangely enough, Roy became mad at me for getting him in trouble so he was more prone to take revenge. At the slightest hint of any backlash I would again scream bloody murder and call for my mom. It was usually at this point I was excused from duty and as punishment Roy would have to finish the chore by himself. For my part, I would disappear down the street to play with my friends.

By the time Roy left for college we both realized our relationship would be forever changed. Even in college he managed to take revenge though. Like the time he came home from college and pinned me between the legs of the television set in our room, leaving me there all night long with a piece of tape across my mouth.

As he matured we became good friends. We voluntarily spent time together. I was even the best man at his wedding. Well, the first one anyway. By the time I got to college I regularly visited him and his wife during any breaks. Although since my parents had moved 1,300 miles away, my options were limited.

When I got married he was the best man and the four of us hung around with each other and took vacations together. My wife and I are even the Godparents to his first child. Amazing how things turned out!

Roy, however, was easy compared to my sisters.

Some friends are the keepers of all nasty secrets. Those secrets that are supposed to remain locked away from civilization for eternity. This kind of friendship is based on unspoken blackmail, as in, "You will remain my friend until the end, or I'll tell everyone about the time you..." These friendships become strained once in awhile.

A few months after my son was born we took a trip back to Montana. I called my best friend from college, Frank, who was a practicing attorney. We agreed to meet for dinner at a local supper club and I introduced Frank to my wife and son.

I should probably mention that Frank was a notorious smart aleck and crude in college but I figured he would have mellowed out a little bit over the past ten years since I'd seen him. I was wrong.

The first words out of his mouth were, "Cute baby, does he look like the father?" The air suddenly thickened to the consistency of cold road tar.

I feigned a chuckle and said, "Very funny, Frank."

My wife however slowly raised her gaze from the baby to Frank and then to me, as if to blame me for Frank's very existence on the planet. I was expecting laser beams to shoot from her eyes and vaporize me for having Frank as a friend. It was going to be a long evening or a very short one, I wasn't quite sure but knew that either way, I was in deep doo-doo.

Later, while we were eating dinner, Frank shot another wisecrack over the bow. I don't really remember what he said but it was enough to trigger a more stinging response. I couldn't resist firing a couple shots of my own.

"Hey Frank, did I happen to mention to you the telephone call I received from the Bar Association? They were asking if I knew anything about a stolen car during our first year of college."

His face dropped. This was kinda fun.

"Oh the ATF called too, they said I might know something about people in the judicial system using marijuana. Are you still smoking marijuana?"

The rest of the evening was pretty uneventful. You could say it was downright quiet. I'm sure that Frank and I are still friends, although we haven't spoken since that night.

Acquaintances are like certain kinds of diet soda. They're sweet, but not nearly as many calories as the real thing.

I stay in contact with a secretary, Trisha, at a previous job I held. She was a hippy in the sixties and never really got over it. You can see it in the way she talks, dresses and fights for every cause you can possibly imagine. I regularly tell her about my latest exploits in the mountains. Her response is always fascinating.

I'll dramatically tell her about some harrowing experience in which I'd almost died and she would respond, "Well good for you. It's so nice to see someone doing something they love. Next time you might want to take a language translation dictionary so you can communicate a little better."

There are some friendships that tend to take a more meaningful turn. This type of friend seems to be sympathetic, loyal, honest, and truly concerned about your well-being.

I have a friend, Aaron, who is well on his way to getting his MBA from a prestigious university. When I dramatically tell him about my latest harrowing experience in which I'd almost died, he responds with a bullet pointed list:

(A) I'm glad you're ok and survived.
(B) I knew I should have given you that crash course in hospital Spanish that I offered in a previous email.
(C) I'm convinced even more than ever that your memoirs are what will make you your fortune.
(D) For your own safety I've applied to the courts for a restraining order. I'm expecting they'll grant my recommendation that you be legally restricted from going anywhere near a mountain. This is both for your safety, and the safety of the mountain. At your current rate of progress, I am fully expecting to get an email someday explaining how you accidentally triggered an eruption in a volcano that had been dormant for 10 million years.

They say men and women can't be friends. Sadly, they may be right. Sometimes friendships between men and women evolve into something that is just not right, especially if one or both of them is married.

Soon after my son was born I brought him to work to show him off to my co-workers. Marcia was holding him and playing with him when I was called to the telephone. Marcia is a woman I've known for ten years. I hired her for a position in my department and sat by as she became my peer and she now is an executive of that same large bank and quite successful.

Anyway, just as I walked around the corner of my office my son was "spitting up" a massive amount of baby stuff. In one quick, deft movement Marcia swooped out her free hand and caught all of the sticky goo. Now if that isn't true friendship, I don't know what else is.

I must confess that my friendship with Marcia is slowly evolving into one of those forbidden relationships. Although she is well aware that I am married, Marcia is a practicing Mormon and believes there is a precedent that makes it okay.

Lately, when I dramatically tell her about my latest harrowing experience in which I'd barely survived, she now responds with, "You are out of control. If you don't stop you're not going to see your son's adulthood achievements, marriage, graduation…"

You see my dilemma? The law only allows for a man to be nagged by one woman.

Because It's There

The one question that seems to be asked of any mountaineer is, "Why do you do it?"

In 1924, George Mallory replied, "Because it's there." Since that time the explanations have grown in veracity and intensity. They even transcend the metaphysical. When I hear these elaborate explanations of why they climb I feel doomed to being a novice. My reason for climbing is because it's been fun and it challenges my physical and mental abilities. I know, I'm so pitiful.

The first question that we need to ask is whether mountaineering really qualifies as a sport. By carefully evaluating the various definitions provided by *The Random House Dictionary* I am confident that mountaineering is truly a sport. The dictionary states that a sport is something subject to the whims or vicissitudes of fate. If that doesn't describe mountaineering to a T, then I don't know what does.

Why do people participate in any sport?

Some people do it for fame and fortune, which we see in the case of football, basketball, baseball, hockey, golf, and women's figure skating. But you'd think that even then those folks must enjoy their sport, at least at some level.

What's worse is that mountaineering is comprised of several different sporting disciplines that require unique skills and abilities and expensive equipment to be competent. This includes rock climbing - the sport of defying the law of physics; ice climbing - the sport of defying the laws of sanity; backcountry skiing - arcanely combining downhill and cross-country ski gear and technique; hiking - the sport of carrying way too much stuff into the mountains; orienteering - the sport of actually getting from point A to point B; glacier travel - the sport of plotting one's way through a mine field; camping -

the sport of sleeping in below zero temperatures and way too much snow, and finally cooking - the sport of trying to eat something at high altitude. Oh, by the way, a mountaineer also has to be proficient in arcane and non-traditional sports such as weather forecasting - the sport of looking at clouds; and avalanche prediction - the sport of digging snow, to make sure they take full advantage of the round-trip adventure. It is unlikely that we'll see any of these sports at the Olympics any time soon. Although, high altitude cooking would make a great spectator event.

I suppose that the sport of mountaineering needs a ball or a puck of some sort. The climber would be required to carry a ball in their hand, or crook of an arm or leg, from the bottom of the mountain to the top. All the while there would be a competing group of climbers that would be knocking rocks and/or ice to bombard the other team. For that matter team members would knock rocks and/or ice on each other. To complicate matters we could throw in inclement weather and avalanches. Oh, wait a minute, that *is* the way it currently works, sans the ball. I guess it's back to the drawing board.

Can you imagine groups of men, women, and children parked in front of their televisions, with an array of snacks, intently watching a small intrepid group of mountaineers scale their way up a peak? Sports bars would be overflowing and patrons would stay for days on end watching the excitement. The media just isn't in tune with consumer needs. If you have any Neilsen's in your neighborhood, try influencing them on this subject.

In recent years there have been quite a few books published about mountaineering. However, many of them are about one single climbing disaster on Mt. Everest. Their dramatic titles certainly cover all the bases: *Air, Climb, Doctor, Woman, My Side, The Other Side,* and of course, *Epic.* For the few people left in the world who haven't written about Mt.

Everest, may I suggest a few possible titles: *Cold, Really Cold, Really Really Cold*, or perhaps: *How to Climb Mt. Everest for the Simpleminded*, or *Climbing Mt. Everest for the Complete Novice*. I'm not sure, but I think that the only people buying books on mountaineering are the authors of mountaineering books. Worse yet, they buy them for research and never really read them. While I've never actually been to Mt. Everest, watch your book store for my soon- to-be-released book, *Climbing Mt. Everest for the Mentally and Physically Impaired*.

In the case of Mt. Everest it completely amazes me that a novice climber would hire a guide and absolve themselves of any responsibility for their own life to climb the highest mountain in the world.

Whatever happened to apprenticing until having sufficient skills and abilities? Guiding one's own destiny?

My wife has carefully analyzed my abilities and has concluded, "You'll climb Mt. Everest over my dead body."

That pretty much sums it up for me. Perhaps I should wear crampons for the first "leg" of the journey – once I save up enough money to hire a guide that is.

I should mention that there are really two types of mountaineers. One has natural ability, strength, prowess, agility, and intestinal fortitude. The dominant trait of the group, to which I subscribe, is that we just don't know when to quit. I may be the only member of this group.

Perhaps the mountaineering community relies too much on disasters. Mountaineers are definitely a different bunch of people, if you know what I mean. Why, you can't pick up a climbing book or magazine without reading the word "epic" at least a thousand times. When these folks get their hands on a word or phrase, that's it, it'll be used in perpetuity (a really long time). As far as the word "epic" is concerned, I don't think that word means what they think that word means. The dictionary says an epic is heroic, majestic, impressively great or unusually great size or extent. The next time I read one of these stories where the authors refers to some "epic" I will substitute the dictionary's definition to figure out what the author is really trying to say.

I imagine it will turn out to be something such as, "My unusually great imagination..." or "in an attempt to generate impressively great fame and fortune from this story..."

Some of the rationale that may explain why a mountaineering author would use a word such as "epic" so often could lie in their very psyche. Just the other day I heard something that aptly describes what I'm talking about. What is the difference between God and a mountaineer? God doesn't think She's a mountaineer.

Without a good (epic) disaster there seems to be precious little fame and no real fortune to be gained. If every mountain climb is an epic then the number of mountaineers would quickly dwindle. The silver lining is that it could stimulate mountain economies – requiring a dramatic increase in search and rescue personnel. Though that doesn't help explain why mountaineers climb. It would seem to be even more of a deterrent. After all, could there really be so many sadomasochists in one sport?

Maybe every mountain climb isn't an epic and maybe we just over use that word. A lot.

Could it be that there is a really simple explanation for why mountaineers climb? I was going to say that it is fun, which would be appropriate based on how the dictionary says that fun provides mirth or amusement. However, fun is too close to make-fun-of, which we all know is to make someone the object of ridicule. In my own experience I have provided a bit of mirth and amusement to my companions as the object of ridicule.

Maybe mountaineers climb because it is enjoyable. Why enjoyable? Because, for some folks, maybe mountaineering is the way they find pleasure - satisfaction marked by accomplishing an objective that requires the full extent of their skill, ability, and experience. On the other hand, it simply could be that a mountaineer climbs a mountain because it's there.

High Altitude Mountaineering: Morality & Leadership

Increasingly throughout the last few years we have heard many explanations for why some high altitude climbers are unable to react to simple moral obligations. Climbing past another person whom they recognize to be in trouble. Giving up on someone as being dead without trying to assist.

The accounts of the 1996 Everest disaster have been well documented from all conceivable angles.

In one account, a journalist writes about being a member of a guided expedition as an observer. It struck me that this author was letting the reader know he was not accepting any responsibility for the events yet to be described. It's like the "prime directive" on *Star Trek*. Don't interfere with the life and culture of alien civilizations.

Before and after each tragic event that unfolds we are given the standard disclosure, "my inability to discern," and, "in my oxygen deprived state," or my personal favorite, "in the guide-client protocol."

Clearly, this author would have been well advised by most parents in dealing with naughty children, "Stop making excuses. What you did was wrong and you need to accept responsibility. If someone gets hurt, it will be all your fault."

We know, scientifically, that the effects of high altitude have a negative impact on the human body. Less oxygen in the air means less oxygen getting to the brain. Less oxygen to the brain means impaired thinking and rationalization.

As an observation, I would offer a response that many a teacher has given me, "That is an excuse, now tell me the reason."

In other words, we look to justify why we do or do not do something.

In this case, we have to ask whether some of these high altitude climbers are looking to justify their immoral behavior by using this as an excuse. We must ask this question because the debilitating effects of oxygen deprivation during high altitude mountaineering do not impact all climbers in the same manner even when faced with the same dilemmas.

There are numerous instances in which high altitude climbers, when faced with life and death situations, have carried out heroics. During the 1996 Everest disaster we saw many instances of compassion and courage.

Certainly, the effects of high altitude mountaineering are serious and should not be minimized or discounted. The mental and physical trauma that a climber must endure is very real and very serious. Is there something more basic and more simplistic to understanding why some climbers behave differently than others?

One possibility is that increased altitude has the effect of revealing our individual essence. Our true self. Like peeling back the layers of an onion.

A person who is self-absorbed or self-centered at their very core is revealed for who they are. Some people create a façade, a false front, in order to deal with people and not reveal too much about themselves. The effects of altitude serve to strip away that façade.

We interact with these people in our every day lives. They are people who think only of themselves and have little respect for others. They're the people who refuse to get involved unless there is a direct and substantial benefit for them. They're disingenuous and feign politeness. We easily see through their façade and know them as being phony.

Luckily, for future of mankind there are other individuals who are generous, giving, and truly care about others. These people are able to instinctively react and come to the aid of a climber in need. The key is that these people don't need to think about their moral obligation, it is just an automatic response.

Goran Kropp[1], in his book *Ultimate High*, summarizes it best.

"In mountaineering, there are several unwritten rules. First is that if a fellow climber becomes injured or hurt, you should do absolutely anything to help that you possibly can. Second, you should never leave a sick or injured climber alone. And third, only in a life-or-death emergency should you save yourself."

Recently, there has been a suggestion that climbers meet a certain level of experience and ability before being permitted to climb certain objectives. Clearly, the sport of mountaineering would benefit from having a certification program that required proven skill levels before a climber is allowed to attempt the many, varying types of conditions. It might even discourage some of these people, who do not have the skills to adequately protect themselves let alone others, who put lives at risk, from climbing.

For these two distinct core personalities, self-centered versus selfless. With which type of person would you rather be acquainted? With which would you rather depend upon in a life or death situation?

A critical factor in all of this is leadership. In guided climbing leadership is most usually bestowed on the most experienced climber and important decisions are deferred to the leaders judgment. Clients subordinate their own judgment and decisions in favor of the guide. This is also a great excuse for those individuals that do not possess the skill, ability, and moral where-with-all, to take responsibility for themselves and their fellow climbing mates.

---

[1] Ultimate High My Everest Odyssey, Goran Kropp and David Lagercrantz. 1997. Discovery Books / Random House. New York. 227p.

In a business environment, we recognize that the leader is not necessarily the most experienced in each facet of the business and that we, as competent employees, must exert influence based on our experience and abilities to ensure quality decisions are rendered. As employees we recognize our responsibility to the business to ensure that it is being well managed to the benefit of its owners, customers and fellow employees. In many cases, this responsibility has legal repercussions. In spite of the passions we bring to our jobs, in most instances, there are no life and death decisions.

Why would anyone ever make a conscious decision to defer all judgment to someone else? In one of the accounts about the 1996 Everest disaster, a client with 33 years of technical climbing experience mindlessly deferred to someone else's judgment. This makes me wonder whether there should be a mental competency test submitted to anyone undertaking such an effort.

Ultimately, climbing is about risk management. Being able to skillfully assess a situation and develop a corresponding plan of action. This is achieved through training and experience. Learning and then applying that knowledge in a real world situation. Not only is each person responsible for their own well being, they are obligated to put themselves into a position of being able to assist others in need.

Anyone who has grown up in a small town or close-knit community understands what it means to look out for others while at the same time looking out for themselves. Those people who are self-centered are usually outcast from the community. Compassion for others cannot be bought, sold, or traded.

The reality is that leadership is a shared discipline. All members of a team must work together in order to accomplish a goal. Each team member has a specific skill set, experience, and personal observations and has an obligation for their own safety and well-being. They must be able to effectively communicate information to the designated leader to ensure a quality decision. The leader, for their part, has an obligation to gather information in order to formulate and execute good decisions. This doesn't mean setting up a committee to consider and debate the minutiae. It does mean that everyone must be observant, willing to contribute, and able to work together to proactively foresee and resolve problems.

Each individual is responsible for his or her own safety, planning, initiative, attitude and required skill set. The leader is responsible for recognizing whether the individual team members actually possess those abilities and skills as well as combining the talents of the entire team to compensate for any shortcomings and arbitrate disputes that naturally arise.

A leader does not have to be the strongest or most experienced climber if each team member accepts personal accountability and responsibility for themselves and their teammates. Each individual has the responsibility for influencing a decision based on practical skills, experience, and abilities that is relevant to a given situation or anticipated chain of events.

The bottom line is that since altitude reveals a persons core morality, a climber should not blindly subordinate them self to another, without a good reason. The ramification of this type of commitment is that each climber must possess the skills and ability for their own safety and success.

As a society we should alienate those individuals that willfully allow another person to die. They should earn disdain rather than fame, praise, and wealth.

To quote Ed Viestures, "Getting there is optional, getting down isn't."

Many of us grew up hearing the phrase, "Be careful in how you treat people on the way up because you just might need their help on the way down."

Morality & Leadership

Helping someone in need is a moral and ethical imperative, not an act of convenience.

*"Fail to honor people,
They fail to honor you.
But of a good leader, who talks little,
when his work is done, his aim fulfilled,
they will say, "We did this ourselves.""*
- Lao-tzu

Aconcagua: Hubris and Humility

Early in life I learned a basic physical law, chiefly that for every action there is an equal and opposite reaction. I've managed to prove the validity of this law in every aspect of my life – sports, work, and love. This is generally a good law to follow, except when combined with other laws such as Murphy's Law. It's kind of like mixing kerosene and an open flame. I reckon this creates a hybrid law – for every good intentioned action there is an equal and opposite negative reaction that must be endlessly repeated in the off chance a positive result can be gained. At least that's the way I feel most mornings as I pry myself out of bed.

Throughout my life my older brother, Roy, has told me that I was adopted. Lately, I'm inclined to believe it just might be true. I have a suspicion that my real parents, the Murphy's, are out there somewhere. Oh sure, they've probably changed their name to something less conspicuous such as Smith, Jones, or Thermopolis, to try and shake the stigmatism that must follow their every action, or reaction, as the case may be.

Sometimes even I am shocked by the events in my life. I do my best to learn from these "incidents" and draw a moral for those unsuspecting poor souls who should be cornered and forced to listen to my stories.

Why just recently I took time away from work to refocus my priorities. I poured so much of myself into my work for so long that I found myself not liking it much anymore. I thrive on pressure and stress. But I wasn't making as much of a difference or driving the level of change I needed.

As is customary for me, I needed some new adventure in my life. I quickly turned to the Internet. Within a short time I had booked a month's worth of mountaineering activities in Western Canada, starting with an ice climbing course and ending with an avalanche certification course. I'd fill the rest of the time with cross-country and alpine skiing. Since this would cover the holiday season, my family would join me for ten days over Christmas for some hearty outdoor fun.

A month after returning, I developed a plan to climb Argentina's Cerro Aconcagua, the highest mountain outside the Himalayas. I had been working on my mountaineering skills for a long time. Although my experience in Canada covered mountains with reliefs up to several thousand feet, I wanted to know how I'd perform at higher altitudes.

After researching Aconcagua I was not really impressed by its reputation. It sees a tremendous amount of traffic each year, with base camp growing to over a thousand climbers at any given point during the peak season. While I don't know how true they are, some accounts indicate that even dogs and motorcyclists have made it to the summit. I resolved myself to the fact that I wouldn't be using any of the hard earned skills I'd learned.

I had chosen to go with a local Argentina guiding outfit that would handle all the logistics of getting me and my equipment to base camp, via mules, and supply the grub. When I arrived in Mendoza I was met by the guide, Ully, and informed there would be seven clients on the trip. There was a Los Angeles physician and his 13-year-old daughter, a project manager from Belgium, a product manager from Ireland, a consultant from France and a Radiologist from Texas, along with myself. The majority of these folks had climbed Kilimanjaro and were making the rounds to the seven summits.

They didn't seem to look upon this climb as becoming one with the mountain to gain the summit through toil and trouble. Rather the mood was like what one would expect in packing up the kids for a day at the beach.

At dinner the first night I realized just how out of place I was. Everyone was talking about how they had porters carry their equipment up "Kili" and there were endless discussions about how delicious the food was, the quality of the wines and coffees they enjoyed. At one point, not having said anything the whole meal, I piped in and told the group that I was used to having to carry my own equipment and that even on guided climbs, I had to help with the cooking, which was only passable at the very best. They looked at me like I was an alien from Mars.

Once we actually began climbing, something I was anxious about doing since my plane touched down, I was reminded at every opportunity just how different I was from the group.

I was in great shape and during all the acclimatization training I was literally running up and down the 12,000 to 15,000 foot levels. I was feeling strong, eating, and drinking well, which is always my biggest challenge at altitude. It was great.

Our day began as soon as the sun would clear the mountaintops which was anywhere from 7:30 to 9:30 am, depending on our location and we would gather in the mess tent for breakfast. If we would be climbing during lunchtime, we would be handed nice little sack lunches as we departed camp.

Each day I would watch the others and evaluate them according to my own novice level of mountaineering experience. Each day they would line up as if in a military march and they would follow in each other's footsteps. If someone was to stop, there was a massive pile-up. It was almost like watching an updated episode of the Keystone Cops. It constantly amazed me how these people found any enjoyment because they couldn't look up from staring at the person's feet in front of them without risking a collision.

It was clear that most of these folks lacked even basic hiking abilities based on how they ascended and descended some of the steeper sections of our trek to reach base camp. I tried pointing out small things such as placing their heels on small rocks as they ascended to take the strain off their calf muscles and they just jeered at me.

On our first rest day after arriving at base camp we hiked to the nearby glacier and donned our crampons.

I was afraid.

As people would walk and climb the various steepness of ice it was clear they held little to no skill level. On a nearly vertical section of ice we needed to traverse in our practice session, I tried to suggest how some folks might plant their ice axe so as to protect themselves in the event they lost their footing. That went over well. They did, however, seem to master the art of sliding down the ice by not planting their crampons correctly.

That night I prayed that no one kill themselves or me. I guess what scared me most was that I was the most experienced climber, with the exception of my tent mate, and I am still a novice.

The more we got into the expedition the more I realized that I was really afraid of what could happen. One thing I knew for certain was that these people couldn't even look out for themselves let alone anyone else. I found myself worrying an awful lot.

It all seemed to stem from my tent mate having a cold earlier in the trip. However for every action… you guessed it, there was just enough incubation time for me to catch his cold as we began carrying equipment to higher camps.

It was absolutely amazing to see how much stuff some of these people were carrying up the mountain. There were two equipment carries, the first day to camp one and the second day to camp two. All of the equipment that was brought to camp one had to be ferried to camp two and the combined loads would have to be carried to camp three and then all the way back down the mountain after summitting. I had a medium sized stuff sack, ice axe and crampons that probably weighed less than eight pounds. The physician from Texas was carrying at least 60 pounds. It was amazing to see it.

He must have owned more goose down than the current population of geese. His plastic boots would have been overkill for a lunar landing. This guy was prepared for a winter ascent of Everest with enough leftover to outfit the Sherpa population living in Nepal. The problem, as I saw it, was that this was the norm for our group.

I think it started one day with an inner ear infection. We carried a load to 16,500 feet and I wasn't feeling well on the descent back to base camp. I'll tell you what, when I started getting ill, I knew things weren't going well. I'd gotten sick at altitude once before because I'd not been eating or drinking enough. In that instance, I chugged down a liter of water and was fine in an hour. This time I had been taking good care of myself and I knew something was wrong. My water intake was more than adequate because I was peeing the Niagara Falls every half hour.

Things had worsened during the night, but I kept telling myself that everything would be fine if I just relaxed and let my body rest. That next morning though, my breathing was shallow, my throat was swollen and sore, there was a sharp stabbing pain in my ear and I had a headache that I thought was going to cause my head to explode.

I asked my tent mate to get Ully. The two of them took me to the medical tent. I knew things were bad. After the doctor put me on oxygen the small tent filled with about eight people all gawking at me and rattling away in Spanish. The one word I recognized that had been repeated several times was Edema. I really hoped they were saying I didn't have it. There are two types of edema and neither of them is a good thing. High Altitude Cerebral Edema (HACE), is marked by swelling of the brain and bleeding which leads to death if the person doesn't descend quickly. High Altitude Pulmonary Edema (HAPE), is marked by the lungs filling with fluid and the person can drown in their own secretions.

The base camp doctor put me on full oxygen and after an hour I had a blood oxygen saturation level of 77 percent. Comparatively, I had been at 83 percent just the day before without supplemental oxygen. My face, hands and feet had gone numb and had swollen up pretty good. My left eye was swollen shut and my head hurt so badly I literally thought it was going to explode.

While we were waiting for the helicopter to arrive they kept telling me to "hang on." Based on what they were saying and what limited knowledge I had of HAPE and HACE, I was beginning to get worried. I say beginning because there was no question in my mind that I wouldn't be okay. I thrive on stress and adversity, remember. I was very emotional when it was time to leave - I didn't want to quit the climb - I didn't want it to end that way.

They had a military helicopter fly in to evacuate me to the trailhead 30 miles away. The helicopter flew about 20 to 50 feet off the ground the whole way, zigzagging in and out of the mountains, so that my condition wouldn't worsen. Once I got down to the trailhead and started back to Mendoza I was completely exhausted. A car was waiting at the trailhead and drove me the 150 kilometers to Mendoza. The roadway winds around a bunch of mountains and the driver was going so fast that the wheels screeched with each curve. I kept thinking to myself that I'd survived HACE only to be killed in a car wreck. There were shrines all along the roadway - for the drivers and passengers that didn't make the curves. I couldn't even raise the strength to talk. I didn't even take off my down jacket - it was easier just to sit and sweat in the 90+ degree temperature.

When we got to Mendoza the driver checked me into the hotel and a doctor was there waiting for me. He didn't speak English and I don't speak Spanish. I pointed and went through the motions of what must have looked like charades on crack. The doctor just looked at me and kept repeating himself in Spanish - like hearing it multiple times was going to finally make a difference to me. The Argentinean doctor at base camp had stuffed a note in my jacket and I handed it to this guy and he handed it right back - it was Doctoreze in a mix of English and Spanish. It would take a group of Egyptologists 50 years to decipher those hieroglyphics. Anyway, this doctor examines me and writes some prescriptions along with a diet for the next few days.

Since my wife is Spanish, I've always relied on her ability to interpret and speak Spanish in the very few instances it's ever been needed. Mainly at Mexican restaurants when living in Arizona, California, and Texas. It's kind of funny how my wife always goes out of her way to speak kindly, in Spanish, to non-English speaking people we've come across. I have a newfound appreciation for being kinder and more considerate to those who struggle in a foreign land. Anyway, I called my wife and spelled the words to her so she could interpret. The prescriptions were a loss but we were able to figure out that the diet was to be bland – rice, apples, carrots, crackers and mineral water. I had the distinct impression that the Spanish-speaking doctor and I hadn't quite connected.

When you've been at altitude your body works to adjust to the thin air and afterwards when you're back at a normal altitude you have all this energy because your body hasn't adjusted to the oxygen rich air. So I'm laying in bed at the hotel feeling sick as a dog and I can't even close my eyes because I have all this energy coursing through my veins. The first night I just lay there hallucinating.

So, here I was in Mendoza, where it was 95 degrees, wearing a heavy down summit jacket, long underwear which had been worn eight days straight at this point and hiking boots - no pants. Luckily my tent mate had thrown some stuff from the tent into my daypack and sent it along. Most of it would have come in handy if I was climbing a mountain, but not a lot of useful everyday stuff for a sweltering summer day in the city. Not that I was going to be going out on the town or anything.

After rummaging around I found a pair of hiking shorts that I had been using along with my old underwear stuffed in a cotton bag as a pillow. If only I had a toothbrush and toothpaste I would have been set for life. I stayed in the hotel for three days and flew back to Dallas. They had sent my gear off the mountain via mules and it arrived just as I was leaving for the airport. What luck.

When I got back to the states my doctor had about ten people in the examination room trying to read the prescriptions and instructions. While I was sitting there he called several pulmonary and neurological specialists who also were mountaineers and they had no clue. They couldn't figure out what the medicines were for. He searched the Internet and found that one of them was used in treating kidney stones (maybe that's what my problem was - High Altitude Kidney Stones). With the next trip he's suggested that I might stockup on some of the important medications so I'm a little better prepared. That seems to be a good idea.

I always wonder why I do this "sport." I have no earthly idea but chances are I'll be at it again. I did learn some valuable lessons about myself and others on this trip.

When I recognized I was in trouble, I had a responsibility to take action even though others might not have agreed, including all the physicians. It's important that each person be self-sufficient to ensure their own safety first. I'm just a country boy from Montana and I'll never be a frou-frou type person nor do I want to be. For me to be successful I need to climb with people who are like-minded, are competent with the required skill set, and have a good attitude toward each other and the mountain.

I'm also sure that I don't know what motivates other people and why someone would take on an objective that is beyond their capability. At least I hope they recognize their skill set for what it is. I guess that there are two ways of looking at this; one type of person doesn't see things for what they are, and the other type sees it but doesn't care. I suppose not recognizing is worse than disregarding. Even though some of these folks made it to the summit, there was too much luck compensating for too little skill. I am happy for those who made it but cannot help but wonder how they view their success.

I would be lying if I said I wasn't a little envious of those who made the summit. I may have not made it but there is always a next time. I will continue on my path of developing a competent skill set. With something that has such dire consequence, I believe it is more important to have skill than luck. Should some situation arise I want to be able to quickly control any problems as well as take advantage of any opportunities.

Looking at it from a completely different angle, the trip wasn't a total bust. My round-trip flight earned 23,000 frequent flier miles. That's enough for one round-trip flight anywhere in the continental U.S. Not too shabby.

My wife hasn't said much about the whole thing, YET, but she's given me my very first list of honey-do's to finish before I can go out to play again.

Intestinal Fortitude

Intestinal fortitude is the ability to finish what you've started. Sometimes this can be as simple as choking down your wife's cooking after she's experimented with some new low fat, high bad taste recipe from a magazine. Or it can be as difficult as doing the right thing against popular opinion, assuming a leadership role, or maintaining integrity in the face of adversity. Our country was founded on the intestinal fortitude of our ancestors fighting for what they believed was right and just.

There are events in my life that have shaped who I am. Some of these events are things that happened directly to me but mostly they have been events that happened to my ancestors, people I care about or know. Leadership and integrity are words that are bantered about regularly in business but they've lost their luster as a practical matter. Doing the right thing in life is often quite difficult and a decision we would rather ignore.

A gruesome act of intestinal fortitude was experienced by my friend's brother, Mike. My friend, Michelle and I were about 11-years-old at the time and Mike was about 16. He had gone deer hunting with his father up in the mountains behind their home. He had tracked a big buck all day long and had even managed to get several shots off but they all missed. When he was down to his last bullet, he downed the deer. Running over to it, he was shocked that it was still alive but mortally wounded. It was bleating, making the sound of a crying baby. Mike was in a real predicament because he didn't have any more bullets and the deer was dying a slow and agonizing death. In an act of desperation Mike ran over to a boulder-strewn slope and gathered a large rock and stoned the deer to death. Michelle and I were playing in their garage when they arrived home. Mike was covered in blood and was crying. He never went hunting again.

This event had a big influence on me and is probably the chief reason that I've never killed an animal on the few occasions I've gone hunting. Having to kill your own food would create a lot of vegetarians.

I often think about what I would have done in that instance. Could I have summoned the courage to do as Mike did or would I have run away?

An example of doing the right thing when it really didn't matter happened when my dad was building a boat trailer out in our garage and my brother Roy was helping. To my young mind the process seemed that they took long heavy pieces of angle iron, cut them with a saw and then welded them back together again.

Roy was holding two pieces of angle iron together while my dad did the welding. Roy had been wearing a heavy long sleeve shirt. It was one of my dad's old gray work shirts. I was standing several feet away watching them, looking through the dark lens of a welder's mask. I remember my dad telling him to hold the pieces still and not to drop them. They were about half done when a piece of molten iron spit out from the welding and landed on Roy's forearm. I watched it as it immediately burned through his shirt, igniting a small flame around the hole. It was all I could do to just point and stammer that there was something burning him. They couldn't hear me yell above the noise of the welder.

In just a few minutes they were done and Roy gently released the newly formed metal on the garage floor and gingerly rolled up the sleeve of his shirt. There was no blood because the molten iron had cauterized the skin as it burned. There was a piece of blackened metal about a quarter inch in diameter, still very hot, imbedded in his skin. He plucked it out and threw it on the floor and was rolling down his sleeve when I again yelled to my dad. Dad took him into the house and doctored him up. When dad told him to stay in the house and relax for the afternoon, I was in a panic thinking that I would be drafted to fill Roy's place. I knew how I'd react if a spark got near me let alone a piece of molten metal. Luckily, my dad worked on wheels and axles the rest of the afternoon.

What's odd is that it didn't matter if he dropped it when he got hit by that molten piece of metal. When I asked, even he didn't know why he didn't drop it. Knowing my brother as I do, he's not a quitter and goes out of his way to finish what he starts. Granted this might be a little extreme but it is a reflection of who he is. I can say in all honesty, that if I'm ever in a life or death situation and need to depend on someone to save my life that Roy would be at the top of the list because I KNOW he wouldn't give up.

To this day, I've never met anyone with the mental capacity to endure so much pain. Whenever I think of my brother I remember that day and shake my head in amazement. Is that guy tough or what?

As a youngster, my father, Richard, went through an unusual bit of circumstances that shaped his life forever. When he was about 20 years old he had, just that day, gone to work for "The Company" as a laborer. The raw copper ore was sent there to be ground-up, melted down, poured into anodes and then shipped by railcar to points all over the world to be converted into pennies, pots, and wire, among other things. It's not quite that simple but you get the point. The town's claim to fame was having the highest smoke stack in the world. When people refer to mining towns as rough and tumble, they really mean it. It takes a special breed of person to work in such a demanding environment where a simple mistake can be deadly.

On my dad's very first day someone had been injured and the medic drafted him to help get the injured man into the ambulance and to drive it to the hospital. It turned out that the man had a massive heart attack and was dead at the scene.

Later that night my dad was out with his friends. He had just bought a car from one of his friend's older brothers and they had gone out on the town to "test drive" it. There were four of them in the car, my dad, two other guys, and a girl. They were on the outskirts of town and it was a dark night. The girl asked my dad if she could drive, and after a while, he relented.

At the same time, unbeknownst to them, the police were chasing a speeding car that was traveling in excess of 90 miles an hour.

As my dad's car was pulling through an intersection the speeding car came careening around a curve in the road and struck his new car broad side. The passenger in the speeding car was hurt pretty badly but the driver was okay. Very drunk, but okay. In my dad's car everyone was fine except him. He had been badly injured. The long thin metal gearshift had impaled him through the side of his chest. His nose and upper lip had been torn from his face and his hand had been sliced open from the tip of his middle finger to the wrist and across all the knuckles.

The policemen who were chasing the car quickly radioed for an ambulance. When it arrived the medic looked at the two injured people and said that my dad would be dead in a few minutes so they took the drunk driver. As they were leaving they told the policemen that they'd be back to retrieve the body.

My father, a little annoyed with their medical prognosis, told the policemen that they couldn't just leave him there all night waiting and that they'd better get him to the hospital. In his usual stubborn way he argued with them over which hospital they should take him to. He wanted to go to Butte, a town 30 miles away. After the policemen debated what to do, they reached in and pulled him from the car, not recognizing that the gearshift had impaled him. As he faded in and out of consciousness he argued with the policemen all the way to the hospital, telling them he'd die for sure if they took him to the one in Anaconda.

Once at the hospital, the doctors sewed his face and hand back together without anesthetic because they didn't know the extent of his internal injuries. They just put a bandage over the chest wound but they thought the internal damage was so massive he wouldn't live very long. Since he had a punctured lung and the air needed someplace to go, his stomach and leg blew up like a balloon. Luckily a specialist in the area came to the hospital, at the urging of my dad's family, and fixed him up. He was in the hospital for three weeks and then went right back to work.

On his first day back at work - his second actual day of work - there was a rather gruesome accident and my dad was again drafted by the medic to help get the injured man to the hospital. He later remembered thinking, "Out of 1,200 men, why do they always pick me?"

This seemed to be an omen of things to come. My dad worked his way through the ranks and studied to become a medic, then an industrial safety nurse and a safety engineer. He believes that as a result of being injured he felt a need to take responsibility for his co-workers and protect them from a similar fate.

Prior to his becoming a safety engineer there were six fatalities a year. Industrial fatalities are more gruesome than you could ever imagine. Even a simple mistake can turn a person into a pile of unrecognizable mush. After he became a safety engineer there were no fatalities. His efforts resulted in virtually eliminating lost-time injuries. He recently told me that he never slept a full night until several years after retiring because he was always thinking about what could go wrong and how he could prevent it.

Now here is a man who gave selflessly and has been a primary example in my life that has helped me deal with adversity and put things into proper perspective when the chips are down.

My great grandparents had a family of five boys and one girl, all rambunctious and most definitely rough and tumble. My grandfather, Willard, was the oldest of the children.

When the children were all quite young my great grandfather contracted a disease called Silicosis that attacked his lungs. It advanced to the point where he was no longer able to work. My great grandmother, fearing for the safety of the children, made him sleep in a room separate from the rest of the house.

My great grandmother couldn't work since she had small children, some still in diapers. Willard, a sixth grader, quit school at 12-years-old and went to work in order to support his family.

After his father passed away, Willard's younger brothers and sister took to calling him Pops. When Willard was around 16-years-old, he forged a letter from his mother signifying he was old enough to work and he applied for a job with the Anaconda Company. When The Company caught on to how old he really was, Willard went into the Navy for a two-year stint. Upon leaving the Navy he was now old enough to return to work at The Company.

What is so amazing is that Willard didn't let adversity keep him down. He was truly a self-made man. He read profusely. His collection of books covered the broad gambit of literature including poetry, fiction, non-fiction and textbooks such as metallurgy.

By the time Willard was 21-years-old he had worked his way up to a position of General Superintendent of The Anaconda Company's foundry operation. They made finished metal products for businesses and governments all over the world. Willard was responsible for 1,800 employees. He could do the job of any employee on the plant mainly because he was the person who bought or built the equipment being used and he took a personal responsibility for knowing every detail of the process.

Willard went on to support each one of his siblings through college. At the same time he married and had a family of his own. Even though he was very successful in his job, his family was the most important aspect of his life. He never owned a house or new car but he successfully raised a large extended family.

There are many success stories to tell that stem from my grandfather. One of his younger brothers went on to be nominated for a Pulitzer Prize and one of his sons went on to be an Olympic caliber ski jumper.

It is through my grandfather's life that I come to realize there is truly a difference between intelligence and education. Here was a man who had everything against him from the very beginning and yet not only did he persevere, he overcame. Not only did he overcome, he succeeded. His success cannot be measure by monetary wealth but rather by the tangible examples of his commitment, values, leadership and integrity.

A person can be educated but not very intelligent. A person can be intelligent but not very educated. The difference being that an intelligent person can become educated but an educated person who is not intelligent cannot become intelligent. In my professional career I see this every day – highly educated people, MBA's, Phd's, etc., who struggle to perform even simple and straightforward work assignments in their field of expertise. How much can be attributed to desire and ambition? What is the personal motivation that drives these people?

There are some events that happened to me personally that also serve to inspire and motivate. Although, in all honesty, I only remember those events in my life that were based on something negative happening. After my Freshman year of college, through an odd set of events, I somehow managed to get a job as a cook at a truck stop out in the middle of the New Mexico desert. I worked for a man, David Martinez, who was a Mexican National and had been living in the U.S. for a few years. My first day on the job I worked the breakfast shift.

My first assignment was to study the menu and become familiar with what the restaurant offered. The first order was for eggs and bacon, which seemed easy enough. When I placed the finished order on the counter and rang the bell for the waitress to pick it up, David grabbed the plate and angrily shoved it in my face. It looked okay to me, although I did break one of the egg yokes and it was leaking around the bottom of the plate and one egg was hanging over the side of the plate a little bit. As he stared at me in utter disbelief he said, "Look at this! Would you eat this stuff?"

As a starving college student, of course I'd eat anything that wasn't completely rotten. Not being a complete moron I knew he was looking for a specific answer of "no."

I knew this was not going to be a pleasant interaction and was not disappointed, when he responded with, "Then why are you expecting our customer to eat it?"

My thought was that anyone who would ever eat at a truck stop would expect greasy food and would not be too concerned about how it was presented. Luckily, my grasp of sanity was still with me and I apologized, promising to do better work. David went on to "explain" that when a customer orders something from the menu they are expecting the food to look just like the picture and to taste better than it looks.

He said that our customers work hard for their money and deserve the best that we can give them.

David then gave me a week to improve my skills or he would fire me. I took his advice and steadfastly held to his words of advice. Later that summer we had a food critic from Albuquerque stop by on his way to a local fishing lake. He was so taken with the quality of food that he gave us a three star rating out of four stars. We were the first truck stop he'd ever even considered rating. Guess who was the cook? Throughout my professional career I've used David's advice and always look to exceed the customer's expectations. After all, it's the customer who pays the bills and keeps the business going.

In my own life I look to the experience of others and use it define my own values and purpose. Very seldom one and the same, there is the easy path in life or the right path.

It seems interesting how the knowledge about our ancestors and other people who touch our lives can have such a profound influence in creating our personal value system. It affects our ambitions and drive to succeed in life. Our intestinal fortitude.

Our ability to be successful in life and business is based solely on our personal motivation that comes from within our own value system. There are so many motivational books written on how to influence others. It seems superficial and self-centered for any one of us to look for someone else, such as a spouse or boss, to motivate us.

Have we become so shallow?

Each of us needs to draw upon the experience of our ancestors, ourselves and the people who touch our lives in order to find honest and true elements of leadership and integrity that we can use to motivate ourselves.

America's success was initially based on the idealistic views of men and women who came to this new world and endured great hardships and suffering in order to achieve freedom. Perseverance is more a way of life than an ideal. Dogged, steadfast, and unyielding in the pursuit of the American dream. Many times the degree of perseverance is in direct proportion to one's level of sanity.

As the early American pioneers traveled westward based on an initial lack of intelligence, their survival was based on ingenuity, desire, and a will to live. There were no social welfare programs, no modern conveniences that we take for granted such as indoor plumbing, electricity, automobiles, tract homes, super markets, or McDonalds. Yet they not only survived, they thrived.

Why? Because they persevered.

I'm sure that when the pioneers headed out from the east coast they intended to reach the west coast and that's why all the land in between got populated.

Pioneers had put up just long enough with all the trials and tribulations of traveling by wagon that they finally picked a spot and said, "We're home!"

You see, they didn't give up, they just persevered long enough to have their objectives change. What were these people thinking, traveling all the way across the continent in wagons that had wooden wheels?

I can just hear the discussion now, "But Pa we're not even half way to California."

"I know son, but just take a look at these wide open plains where the deer and the antelope roam. Why I can't even hear a discouraging word."

"Think about how wonderful it would be to live here and toil in the fields and endure droughts in the summer and numbing cold and snow in the winter. Sure we could go on to California where there is nothing but smog, horrendous commutes and the food looks pretty but tastes something awful."

"Gee Pa, you're right, lets stay here."

People who stand still won't stub their toes but they also don't make much progress. None of us likes to make a mistake especially a painful one. It's interesting to see that those people who are truly successful in business, sports, or life in general, have made too many mistakes to even count. Rather than chalking it up as a complete loss they try to learn something from it that will improve their judgment or skill set. Rather than give up they keep going.

Consider the following individual who was a folksy man with an incomparable sense of humor. This man was devoted to his country and the welfare of all its citizens. He actively displayed morality and ethical values and was a model of honesty and integrity. Despite tremendous adversity he accomplished great things. The number of failures outnumbered his successes but he still somehow managed to ascend to the pinnacle of success. Following is a list of events that he realized at different stages of his life:

Age
22   Failed in business
23   Ran for legislature and was defeated
24   Failed in business
25   Elected to legislature
26   Sweetheart died
27   Had a nervous breakdown
29   Defeated for Speaker
31   Defeated for Elector
34   Defeated for Congress
37   Elected for Congress
39   Defeated for Congress
46   Defeated for Senate
47   Defeated for Vice President
49   Defeated for Senate

51   Elected President of the United States

This is the record of Abraham Lincoln[2]. He was a leader who made hard decisions to break the bonds of slavery. He harbored ideals that would cost him his life. He is the epitome of what it is to be an American. He never quit fighting for what was right and just.

I hold "Honest Abe" in the highest regard for his achievements to the extent that I have even patterned certain aspects of my life as a result of things he did. For example, I would never go to a play. If for some reason my wife were to force me to go I would never sit in the balcony unless of course it didn't cost anything extra.

Although, I've learned that Abe refused to appoint Ulysses S. Grant to head up the Union army until Grant agreed never to run for president against Abe.

Even the mighty ones have chinks in their armor.

Who knows, maybe there's even hope for me!

---

[2] Bits & Pieces. Vol. M / No. 3. The Economics Press, Inc.

Flying

When I was a small child it was a big deal to ride in an airplane. In fact I had never even known anyone who'd gone up in an airplane. When my family traveled the 28 miles from our home in Anaconda to Butte to spend the day, we would regularly park at the airport and watch the planes take off and land. Due to the high mountain range that surrounded the narrow valley, the planes had to take a steep angle in and out of the airport. It was so exciting to even dare think about flying.

When I was about 12-years-old my father, who was 30-something at the time, had to attend a training school in Chicago. We took him to the airport. There were so many mixed emotions as he walked across the tarmac to the airplane and climbed the stairway. I was joyous that he was finally able to go up in one of those contraptions, afraid of what might happen, and envious of him too. I was convinced that my dad was a true daredevil.

It was at this point I discovered that one of my goals in life was to become a pilot. Not just any kind of pilot mind you, I envisioned my collection of airplanes would include a military fighter jet to save America from the Russians, a large passenger jet to take my family on vacation to hot spots around the world and a bush plane that I would need for my livelihood as a mountain man. I figured the diversity of airplanes would keep me covered no matter what my needs would be. Since my mother was afraid of flying, I figured we would just tie a long rope to my wagon and we'd pull her along behind us.

As I grew, went off to college, and then acquired a wife, a mortgage, car payments, and a child, my goal of becoming a pilot slowly faded into the background.

A few years ago I had taken a job in Atlanta with a large multi-national company. Within a short time I discovered that management above me were doing things that I deemed as not kosher. Rather than move my family, I chose to commute from our home in Dallas. I would leave home on Sunday evening and return on Friday evening. I promised my wife and son that I'd either find a way of making enough change for the job to be palatable, find a new job, or quit and stay home for a while. During the subsequent two years I logged over 300,000 miles on commercial airplanes. Most of the time my flights departed reasonably on schedule but there were many occasions when I had to re-route my flight due to weather or broken planes. Amazingly I never missed one day of work and was always home on Friday. Sleep, however, became optional.

I was finally able to convince my boss to let me work from home. In all his graciousness, he let me work from home one week each month. My first week working from home happened to be the week that terrorism struck America. September 11, 2001.

It was at this point I reassessed my life. My job in Atlanta wasn't improving because the guy I worked for was making business decisions solely on how he could benefit financially, and as a result the business languished. My peers were content to just ride it out and were banking on the fact that the parent company had deep pockets and a reputation for never firing anyone for any reason.

And I felt guilty for being away from home so much.

My wife was essentially a single parent and my son always asked when we could live together again. In addition, while the odds of being in an airplane accident are worse than winning the lottery, I was buying enough quick-picks that I was concerned about being in the wrong place at the wrong time. As a result, I fired my boss, which effectively freed up my career options and permanently returned me home to Dallas by mid-October.

My birthday is in October and for a present my wife purchased an introductory flying lesson. Given the proximity of the events of September 11, I wasn't quite sure what message she was trying to send me. I always thought she was joking when she told me to jump off a cliff but it seems she really wants me to become airborne. Maybe something Freudian was happening? Given the huge career change I had just undergone, maybe she thought I needed to mentally deal with my demons or something, although I have enough demons to keep the horror film industry alive and well for years to come.

Previously, the total extent of my personal flying skills was limited to take-offs and landings that were very close to the ground.

As kids, my friends and I would ride our bikes and pretend we were Evil Knieval, jumping logs, creeks, cars and each other. Our brief encounters being airborne usually involved gear up crash landings that would send one of us to the infirmary for doctor mom to patch up. Over time our landing skills never really improved, our supply of bicycle parts was exhausted along with the patience of our parents, and we were forced to halt our test flights.

More recently, I was rock climbing in the Lake O'Hara area of western Canada with another fellow. I was holding a rather large piece of shale and admiring its geological properties. It was gray, with sharp edges and about the size of a loaf of bread. Of particular interest to me was how this rock had broken cleanly away from the overall formation. I had been clinging to this particular piece of rock and since both the rock and I were several hundred feet off the ground the pull of gravity instantaneously took affect. After quickly calculating my rate of descent at 32 feet per second - per second, I determined the approximate length of time in which life, as I knew it, would continue to exist. Even though it was a re-run, I had just enough time to watch my life flash before my eyes.

While the performance would never earn an Oscar - Hollywood is so finicky - the story line and raw emotion of the lead actor almost made me cry at the end.

The fellow I was climbing with hadn't been placing the most solid rock protection during this climb so I hadn't placed much hope on it. Several times, during this particular climb, when I would clear an obstacle there would be some piece of protection that would come rocketing down the mountain attached to a carabiner along the climbing rope, aimed straight for my head. I wondered how long, measured in milliseconds, he could hold onto the rock before my falling weight would pull him off. As luck would have it the protection held and the dynamic climbing rope stretched like a bungee cord and a G-force of about 20 gently slammed me into the rock wall below causing my body to resemble a fair imitation of a pancake covered in strawberry jam.

The airport my wife selected for my aviation baptism is almost in the heart of Dallas in the midst of tall buildings. The airplane was a Cessna 150 that seemed to be approaching terminal depreciation. As the instructor walked around the aircraft going through the preflight checklist, I obediently followed along as he hunched over and looked intently at each moving part. The clearance under the wings of this particular aircraft is about 5 feet 5 inches. Since I am 5 feet 8 inches the trailing edge of the wing was the perfect height for striking me right in the forehead when I blindly walked into it.

Once in the plane the instructor started it up and taxied to the runway. The take off was exhilarating. The instructor chose to take me to a practice area over farmlands bordering Oklahoma. I figured that the flight out there would give me just enough time for my vision to return and the throbbing pain in my forehead to subside.

After showing me how to get the aircraft to go up and down and turn right and left, the instructor turned the controls over to me. At 3,000 feet off the ground traveling at 100 miles per hour is like waiting for a bus that never comes. We're talking slow. The scenery doesn't seem to change at all. After increasing the altitude and making a left turn I then decreased the altitude and made a right turn. After several variations of altitude changes and turning the airplane I was convinced that even I could learn to fly.

On our return to the airport, the instructor resumed control of the aircraft. As we approached for our landing, there was all kinds of chatter from the airport control tower. They were granting permission to all kinds of aircraft to land and I was concerned as to how they kept track of who was landing, and in what order. When I questioned the instructor about how they could give all of us permission to land at the same time he indicated that there were jets landing that traveled a wee bit faster than us and that they would probably park the plane and drive home by the time we reached the airport.

The landing itself was quite unique. Because there was a cross wind, the instructor approached the landing strip at a right angle rather than straight on. As the plane grew closer to the ground our angle straightened out until we were about at a 15-degree angle. It felt like we were landing sideways. Once we taxied away from the runway the instructor stopped the plane and began fumbling with the radio. It turns out that radio reception had cut out on our approach to the airport. Once he was able to restore two-way communication with the tower we learned that they could hear everything transmitted by the instructor and we just couldn't hear them.

Given my track record with take-offs and landings, this experience has helped to diminish my enthusiasm about becoming a pilot. Left on my own, there's no telling what could have happened.

Although I should probably embrace the idea of becoming a pilot because there's no telling what's up my wife's sleeve for my next birthday present. She has mentioned something about boating, perhaps I should get started and learn about survival at sea and medical advances for drowning victims.

Guardian Angels

When my grandfather passed away everyone in the family thought that my grandmother would not be far behind since they were each other's life. That was 26 years ago. My grandmother, Irma, is without a doubt one of the most fascinating people I know.

At last count she has 11 children, 28 grandchildren, 56 great grandchildren and 16 great-great grandchildren. All of them still living. At birth, Grandma writes each of our names down in her bible. Every day she says a prayer for each of us, which takes her about two or three hours. You could say she is a spiritual person but not a fanatic or a zealot.

Every year for as long I can remember, Grandma has entered her knitting and crafts in the county fair. Each year she brings home a stack of blue ribbons. And each year she says that she won't compete again. She is a volunteer for the local library where she reads every book and decides whether it should be made available. She'll stay awake reading until 3:00 am every night. We tease her about reading all the romance novels twice, "Just to make sure."

While some of her offspring have been affected by serious illness, no one has died. Given the number of people in her family, this would seem to be a statistical anomaly.

Several years ago when my grandmother was a young 84, she was a passenger involved in a bad car accident. Much to the amazement of her doctor and family, only her knee was injured, which caused her to slow down and not attend quite so many dances at the senior center. When she was 89, she began suffering from problems with her vision, dizziness and muscle coordination. We all thought that old age had finally arrived to claim her. After several tests her doctor found a brain tumor about the size of baseball in the back of her head.

Because her mobility was compromised, every day the priest would arrive at her house to pray with her. The priest would tell her that she had lived a long and fruitful life and it was now okay to let go and be at peace. The prognosis from her doctor was bleak and her advanced age prohibited all of the standard treatments. However, my grandma had two hands still firmly grasping life and wasn't about to let go. Grandma's condition steadily worsened and she became wheelchair bound. Relatives, now spread from here to kingdom come, began making the pilgrimage to see Grandma, expecting it to be the last. Yet, through all of this, Grandma persevered.

Grandma was admitted into the hospital with increasing regularity. One night, about two years after being diagnosed with the tumor, we received a telephone call from my mother that Grandma was in the hospital and, "things didn't look good." This code was deciphered to mean that we should begin packing for the funeral. But, as usual, within a few days Grandma was released from the hospital and sent home.

Since that point in time my grandma's condition began to improve. First her vision improved and then the dizziness went away. Medical tests indicated that the tumor seemed to be getting smaller. Eighteen months later the doctor told her that the tumor was gone.

She'll occasionally use a walker at home and my mom insists she use the wheel chair when they go shopping. I think my mom wants to use the wheel chair mainly to push people out of her way to make a path to the sale racks though.

I can honestly say that I believe that either my grandma willed her tumor away or whomever she is praying to has some good connections. The latter would seem to be the most likely option given how the rest of us have fared. At 97, grandma is as sharp as a tack and has a great sense of humor. She is the epitome of mind over matter.

My schoolmates haven't fared nearly as well at succeeding with life though. My very first experience with death was in the third grade when one of my best friends, Kenny, died from chicken pox. Later, when I was a high school sophomore a classmate, Marty, died of bone cancer. I think about my friends often and wonder how their lives might have turned out differently if they'd just been given a chance. I've wanted to call their families just to say that I remember their children and hold their memories dear to my heart. But I don't because I don't want to dredge up painful memories for them.

In the 20 years since we graduated high school about half of my wrestling teammates have died either by their own hand or killed by someone close to them.

Lenny was married just six months when he and his wife went flying in a small plane owned by a friend. The plane malfunctioned, or something, and crashed in the mountains of western Washington.

Geno had taken Scott's car keys away from him at a party because Scott was too drunk to drive. Scott was walking home down the middle of a usually deserted roadway when he was run over and killed. Apparently Geno blamed himself for years. Then one day, Geno was driving home drunk when he hit a little girl riding her bike. He thought he killed her and went home and shot himself. It turned out that the little girl was fine.

Lee was working in Alaska and one long dark winter's day decided that he couldn't take it any longer and shot himself.

Steve was out hunting with his father. It seems they were out west of town hunting and his dad heard a noise coming through some brush, shot into the brush and ended up shooting Steve in the chest.

With the passage of time my friendship with these guys seems to increase and the tensions and disagreements seem so trivial. I think about these friends and wonder how their lives could have taken such a tragic turn. What could have been done differently to give them a future, to give them hope? Why are so many bad things happening to such a small group of people?

I also wonder why I've been spared so often. My ski accident in high school seemed to be the first of many near misses.

When I was 22-years-old I had already been married a year. I was attending college full-time and working full-time as a warehouseman for an electrical distributor in Albuquerque. One day I was sent out on a job, taking a big flat bed diesel truck to a job site to pick up a load of metal pipe. Each piece of pipe was ten feet long, about ten inches in diameter and weighed 200 pounds. The whole stack of 30 pipes was bound together with metal bands.

When I arrived at the job site, there was a crew of about four men ready to load the pipe on my truck. A big diesel powered forklift came over and lifted the pipes and brought them over to the truck. I was standing on the truck bed and the others were down below guiding the bundle into proper position. As the forklift raised the bundle a few feet over the truck bed I noticed that the forks were stuck into the bundle rather than neatly underneath it. This meant that the metal bands holding the bundle together were bearing the load of the pipes versus the forklift. My immediate thought was that I hoped the bands held. Just as soon as that thought struck, one of the bands broke with a loud ping. One end of the heavy pipes slammed down. Then the other band broke, sending the full weight of the pipes onto the truck.

In a fraction of an instant I could see one of the pipes was swinging straight for the head of a worker standing next to the truck. His attention was focused on the other direction. Without thinking I threw myself into the fray of pipes so that my body would stop the pipe from decapitating that guy.

Ouch, that hurt. I was hit across the lower back and hips but it had served to stabilize the pipes. At this point I wasn't feeling too well and let the workers finish loading the truck.

The next day at work I was moving slow and not able to stand up straight or bend over. At the end of the workday, the warehouse manager sent me home and told me to get examined by a doctor. As it turned out that would be my last day of physical labor. I had three cracked vertebrae and two previously fused herniated discs that had gotten screwed up in high school.

I spent the next year and a half in and out of the hospital (mostly in) and endured several surgeries. The biggest operation was to permanently fuse the three vertebrae together. The surgery was to start at 7:00 am and last four hours. The surgical team arrived early that day so they were able to get started at 6:00 am. Due to complications, I was wheeled out of surgery and into the recovery room 16 hours later.

One doctor had nicked my spinal cord, permanently damaging it, which caused a loss of sensation in some of my toes. The orthopedic team couldn't harvest enough bone from my hips to use in fusing the vertebrae so they got a bunch of bone from a cadaver to finish the job. This was a new experience for me to consider - having some dead person's bone implanted in me.

At one point I went into cardiac arrest and they had to use a defibrillator to revive me. For more than two years after that I couldn't allow anything to touch the square spots on my chest where the defibrillator had been used. Even in the shower the water would cause an intense burning, searing pain.

Since that time, my wife has a habit of thinking up dangerous new sports that "we" should try out. It often starts with, "Wouldn't it be neat to..."

After 19 years of marriage I should begin to learn my lesson.

While we were living in Albuquerque, Carrie had the bright idea that we needed some bicycles so we could get outside and get into better physical shape. A week later I, along with my new racing bike, entered a 100-mile bicycle race through the Rio Grande Valley. The last five miles I had to get off and walk because my legs couldn't move enough to complete the pedaling action. Although, sheer willpower let me finish in the top half of the field. After recovering I developed a program and was riding 300 miles a week. One evening, just before sunset, I was taking a short 20-mile bike ride. As I was coming down a hill at about 30 miles an hour, a small white car pulled across the lane in front of me and I struck it broadside. The impact of my body mangled the door and both front and rear fenders on the passenger side. My head hit the side window, bursting it into small little square shaped shards.

As I lay there waiting for the ambulance to arrive I had some time to think since moving wasn't really an option and I was breathing only when absolutely necessary. It struck me as odd that Carrie's bright idea could be so potentially dangerous. She hadn't even taken her bike out of the garage more than a few times and hadn't even logged ten miles on it since she'd owned it.

After spending a week in the hospital and then a week on the couch at home recuperating, I decided that cycling probably wasn't the sport for me.

Since that time, a pattern has developed in which Carrie comes up with a brilliant idea for some new sport "we" should try. Somehow I become completely enveloped by her idea, obsessed, if you will. Carrie, for her part, sits idly by, encouraging me. When I ask her to participate, she always replies with, "Oh no, you go ahead and get good at it and then you can teach me."

One of these days I'm going to have to check out the life insurance policies that keep showing up in the mailbox.

I do wonder why I've survived all of these accidents. Heck, it's even a miracle that I've survived most of the cures. Through it all I've come to develop a belief that there is a guardian angel watching out for me. After all, I couldn't be that lucky. Okay, so it could be that repeated severe head trauma can cause delusions and impaired mental functions, but I take great comfort in knowing that Grandma is saying a prayer for me every day. With her connections I stand a fighting chance of growing old.

My wife has a saying that God watches out for children and fools. We've been married so long you'd think she would stop thinking of me as a child.

Risk Management

Risk management is the science of analyzing data and making decisions based on a sound and logical methodology. Risk is the element of unknown in a decision. The level of risk in making a decision where some of the facts are unknown can sometimes be deadly and at other times be inconsequential. Obviously, the amount of the unknown needs to decline in direct proportion to the increasing significance of a decision. To put it another way, risk is the leap of faith one takes after weighing the consequences of a decision.

As a kid my parents worked to instill in me the ability to recognize and manage risk. Most often these were If / Then statements followed by words of support such as, "If you put your hand on that hot stove you'll burn yourself and when you do, don't come crying to me."

My brother, recognizing my parent's risk adverse nature, tried very hard to get me to embrace risk. He was certainly more encouraging than may parents. During winter he would often tell me, "Go stick your tongue on that fence pole." Or, "I bet you could jump from the roof of the garage into that pile of snow."

In school, teachers are effective in training us to remain stoically silent while observing work that is being performed incorrectly. This is known as the tattletale rule. This is an especially useful tool in the real world when, after days or weeks, the work has to be redone, assuring job security. Of course the value of job security far outweighs the fact that the rework is three times the original cost.

I'll often ask myself, "Self, what information do I really need to make this decision? What pieces don't I have? What are the different consequences that can occur if I make the decision without having that information? What is the likelihood of those consequences, particularly the negative ones, occurring?"

I do try to hold these conversations in my head so as not to unnecessarily alarm anyone that my mental state might be a few degrees off plumb. A I grow older and repeatedly lose to myself, my debate skills are steadily improving.

One can logically assess the unknown by identifying the various "what if" scenarios – things that could happen. By example, you are driving down a dark street during a heavy thunderstorm and you come to an intersection where the streetlight is not functioning.

The element of unknown is: 1) if you drive through the intersection, would you collide with another vehicle driving along the cross street? 2) If you stop at the intersection could you be struck from behind?

You may believe that becoming involved in an accident is a low risk, but if it happened, the costs would be high. Someone could be injured or killed and at the very least there would be damage to a vehicle that could lead to increased insurance premiums. As a precaution, you'd probably gather as much information as possible by looking out your windows and checking your mirrors. Most likely, you'd begin to slow down, maybe light your emergency flashers. Once you've fully assessed the danger from the cross street and the traffic behind you, then you make a decision on a proper course of action. Do you stop? Where do you stop? How quickly do you stop?

In other words, you assess the risk of something bad happening to yourself and to others. You then weigh the probability of something bad happening against the amount of damage that could occur if it did happen. If the probability is low, but the amount of damage is high, then you'd certainly want to be cautious. You'd still keep going but maybe you'd slow down well in advance of the intersection to avoid being rear-ended or stop at the intersection to let opposing traffic proceed.

The idea here is not to avoid the risk but to take precautions against something bad happening when you do take the risk. It is reducing the element of the unknown in your decision making process.

Most people think that managing risk means avoiding taking any risk. But as the prior example illustrates, the challenge is to take risks based on sufficient information so that precautions can be taken against something bad happening.

When I tell people of my chosen profession as a risk manager they seem quite surprised.

The usual response is a wide-eyed, "Oh, really."

Immediately followed up with, "And you climb mountains?"

As if my job and hobby are diametrically opposed, like good and evil. Although, my record of injuries makes one wonder about my ability to quantify the negative consequences of risk. My response is that in my chosen athletic endeavors I view death and/or dismemberment as the negative consequence and anything short of that is an acceptable risk. If I manage to live through the metamorphous and become a real mountaineer then my level of acceptable risk would diminish.

Being able to gauge risk, especially in a timely manner, is a function of experience.

Why?

Because by doing something wrong enough times you eventually figure out how to do it correctly and avoid the pitfalls. In my line of business, the most successful risk managers have a tremendous amount of practical experience, most often gained by working up through the ranks and then being re-trained to be unbiased and analytical. In other words, these people have made every mistake in the book. Luckily they are smart enough not to make the same mistake twice.

The risk manager is usually the person who is in the middle of the path between a person's brilliant idea and the implementation of that brilliant idea. Unfortunately, it is human nature for people to come up with an idea and then force their will upon others until they get their way.

A business is usually divided into warring factions, called departments, which have opposing performance objectives and goals. The marketing and sales people get incentives to sell more product. The finance group is challenged with reporting increasing sales, profit, and ultimately reducing expenses to earn more money for the owners and investors. The operational groups always want more staff and technology. In many businesses people tend to do things based on emotion. They want it because they want it.

My favorite statement came from a senior marketing manager, "If it was a bad idea, I wouldn't have thought of it."

These folks couch their personal opinion in terms such as customer feedback so it doesn't seem so obvious, but having real, tangible information is important to support a conclusion. If the risk manager doesn't automatically agree that someone's brilliant idea isn't the best thing since sliced bread, they are usually demonized, vilified, and subjected to brute force influence, intimidation, bad-mouthing, name-dropping, death threats, and all other sorts of proactive measures. The most obvious sign of a bad risk manager is that someone other than his or her boss likes them.

I've had the opportunity to work at some of the largest financial institutions in the country. The funny thing I've noticed is that my thought process and business decisions have been viewed as conservative in one area of the country and liberal in another. Even though my job is essentially the same and I deal with the same types of problems. The only difference is the people.

Not too long ago I had taken a new job in Atlanta, and since I agreed to start immediately, I negotiated some time off to be taken after three months, so that I could take my regularly scheduled semi-annual climbing trip and family vacation. I was planning on climbing some near 14,000-foot mountains in southwest Colorado.

By the time I was ready to leave for my trip, I was already heavily entrenched in a number of projects, from revamping operations to launching new products. To make sure I wasn't the cause for any lose of momentum in getting work completed, I scheduled time when I would make myself available to teleconference on important issues. My first availability would be five days after leaving for vacation. I would be back in civilization after a climb where I was to summit three peaks that involved some extensive backcountry hiking, and climbing rock, snow and ice.

All went well until our fourth day, when we were fooled by the weather as lightening storms threatened to move in earlier than expected. Within minutes of reaching the summit dark storm clouds formed. At our altitude of 13,800 foot the storm clouds were literally overhead. We quickly gathered our equipment and headed down the mountain on the double-quick. Our ice axes started a high pitch humming noise as we began descending the snowfields. This was a very ominous position we were in, carrying a metal ice axe in one hand and metal crampons on both feet. It is surprising how quickly one can move when one knows they're a human lightening rod.

While I didn't feel particularly intelligent in getting caught like that, I was comforted in knowing there are people with even less common sense than I. After all, how could some poor pitiful golfer ever let himself get into the position of getting struck by lightening? All they have to do is put down their golf club and climb into the cart where the rubber tires of the cart will protect them.

By the time we made it back to camp it had begun to hail. The temperature at camp dropped from 75 down to 29 degrees in less than a half hour. Over six inches of hail fell within an hour. As lightening flashed all around us I would try to count the seconds until hearing the boom of thunder but it was always instantaneous. The entire time we squatted on our sleeping pads. I rocked back and forth on the balls of my feet to try and take my mind off the numbing pain from being hunkered down like that. We ended up waiting for about three hours before the storm blew over and we were able to relax. By that time my body was locked in a sort of cramped convulsion. I would have welcomed being struck by lightening in the hope that it would knock me over and get me out of that fetal position. I was certain that the lightening would have hurt less.

By late afternoon on the fifth day we were comfortably back in Durango. After a quick shower, I was just in time for my conference call with the office where there was a cast of thousands in the room.

The head of product development, Renee, had been arguing with one of my staff members about beginning a project, a brilliant idea that would make the company millions. After asking a few basic questions, it was clear the idea hadn't been well thought out.

Not wanting to admit that we needed more work on the idea before pouring our human and financial resources into it, Renee chose to go on the attack, "I understand you are a very risk averse person but you really need to think outside the box."

I was speechless, for so many reasons. The conference room had gone silent and after a few moments I said, "Could someone explain to Renee where I'm at and what I'm doing."

Managing risk is about making an informed decision based on collecting the right facts and applying the right knowledge. At least one of the largest companies in the world has a philosophy that managers don't need to have practical experience with the work they are supervising. This company has a sales culture where people advance based on their ability to sell a product to customers and themselves to management. This seems like a brilliant idea. I'm adamantly opposed to it.

If you needed a surgical procedure, would you choose a doctor with a proven track record who has successfully performed that particular procedure many times or a doctor who was a really nice person but had never done that procedure before?

Now, continuing along this example, let's think about the company that makes the surgical equipment, such as complex electronics and nuclear medicine. If your life depended on the quality of the surgical equipment being used, what kind of people would you prefer build it? Who would you want managing the people who build it? It seems like a pretty simple decision.

When it comes to managing risk, what kind of person would you want working to take an idea through to final product? For a brilliant idea on a new piece of surgical equipment?

Team dynamics, whether in a work environment or sports setting, are affected by the experience, knowledge, skills, ability, and personality of the participants. There is no one area more important than another. Someone with a great personality who has no experience, basic knowledge, skills, or ability will drag against the team's success. Conversely, someone with extensive experience and complete knowledge, skill and ability can also cause a drag on the team's success based on their personality.

Personality is the glue that binds a team together. The basis of a team's success is the quality of experience, knowledge, skill and ability of each team member. Nevertheless, it doesn't need to be identical for each team member. Based on the objective of the team, each person should have a complimentary and supplementary overall skill set. We've all heard this before in terms of the whole being made up of the sum of its parts.

Each person on a team has the responsibility to do his job to its fullest in support of the team's objective. If one person does not have the skill or ability, then the risk is that a portion of the team's work is either not completed or only partially completed.

When it comes right down to it, everyone manages risk everyday of his or her life. Sometimes we get trapped in our own little niches. It's always easier to criticize than to look at the big picture and use our abilities to compliment and supplement those of our teammates. Sometimes you have to go outside the box in order to really think outside the box.

Kings and Princes

There are so many kinds of personalities out there that it is really tough to figure some people out. Basically there are three types of personalities that we should all be concerned about.

1. People you like
2. People you don't like
3. People you neither like nor dislike

Personalities change according to the people we hang out with. When I was in school, none of my friends really had a personality to speak of so there was nothing to rub off onto me, either good or bad. That's not to say that my friends and I didn't do our share of not-so-nice things such as that panty raid during our freshman year of college. I learned a valuable lesson with that one. Don't steal all their underwear and don't throw it all in one bag.

Of all my friends though, I'll make it very clear that I was the most sweet, innocent, and upstanding person in the group. I am almost sure that the fact I am the one writing this story bears no influence on the historical facts. If any (former) friend chooses to dispute my description of myself, they are wrong.

Because I've spent so much time at work, the people I've befriended were the people that I worked with. I was probably most influenced by my bosses. The impact they had on my sense of humor and personality are the reason why many companyies now have mental health programs.

When I got into banking, I worked for a crusty old broad, Karen, who had a real no-nonsense management style. She could detect uncertainty at fifty yards and could unleash a well-aimed cynical and snide remark with the precision of a smart bomb. Unfortunately, my retorts were of the scud variety, deadly if they hit their target but with such a poor guidance system that they almost always blew up mid-flight. Karen is the female equivalent of Don Rickles, just not as empathetic and nurturing.

I had a job interview for a risk management position at a large division of an even larger bank. The hiring manager, Terry, was someone who I couldn't get a read on his personality. The things that he said and the way he said them could be taken as either insulting or as a dry sense of humor. Sitting there listening to him, I couldn't believe that someone could be that mean spirited, so I chose to believe he just had a dry and very wry sense of humor. So, when he'd say something, I'd laugh. I figured that if I laughed at his remarks he'd either think I was a complete idiot or that I was someone who understood his sense of humor.

I got the job.

Although it took me awhile before I could tell the difference between when he was joking and being serious. They were so similar. When he'd physically show signs of being mad and offer more pointed expletives directed at me, I'd know he was being serious. Sometimes I'd even remember to stop laughing, which seemed to help.

While living in Phoenix, I worked for a woman, Robin, who had wit, intelligence, and an addictive sense of humor that always brought everyone into agreement with her point of view. At work we were an inseparable team, I would come up with the plan and the details, and she provided the muscle to get it approved. During a time when the bank was on an acquisition spree, we would often work up to 20 hours a day on the conversions. There would be times, late at night, when we would be so punchy from the stress and lack of sleep that we would just start laughing uncontrollably about the most stupid things such as signing our names to documents. At one point she told a co-worker that she wanted to have an affair with me but refrained from propositioning me because, "He'd tell."

I was a bit perplexed when a few months later she divorced her husband of 20 years and ran off with another woman. I often wonder where exactly I fit into her conversion from one "team" to the other.

I once worked for a guy in Des Moines who was as anal retentive as one could get and a dedicated smoker. Whenever he was not in his office he could be found sitting in his car, smoking. I regularly had to walk out to his car in the parking lot in order to meet with him. On one occasion I even had to make a presentation to him in the cab of his pick-up truck for his approval on a $15 million expenditure. In the dead of winter you'd see him traipsing off through knee deep snow, in below zero weather, without a coat, to his truck for a smoke break and a nap. When I'd ask him how he could possibly handle walking around outside without a coat he would reply, "Mind over matter, if you don't mind, it don't matter."

As a result of managers I've had the privilege (or misfortune) of working for during my early and mid career, I've developed my own rather unique traits. Having unique traits is important for any person but I have found that the higher one climbs the corporate food chain, the more unique their personality needs to be.

I'm the kind of person who people either love or love to hate. There are even some people who love to hate me. Little do they know that kind of attitude just fuels me even more.

Growing up in a large family, disputes were not uncommon, and I've carried many of those negotiation skills into my career. Although, I never get to hit anyone anymore.

I was never one to strike permanent political alliances. Instead I always chose to go with who I believed was right. This way it was easier than trying to defend a position that was wrong in order to pay somebody back.

My father was the, "Speak softly and carry a big stick" kind of person. His stick happened to be a wide leather belt. Having developed way too much quality time with my father's belt, I once drew the courage to sneak it into the garage and proceeded to cut it into tiny little squares. To cover the crime, I doused the pile of leather bits with some kerosene and burned it to a crisp. To finish it off, I buried the ashes about 120 feet deep in my mother's vegetable garden.

Anytime I meet a group of new people either at work or in sports, I tell everyone upfront that they can either choose to believe that I have a sense of humor and take my comments in that light, or they can believe I am a complete jerk. In either case, they will be right. The perception they choose to hold will yield the precise results they are looking for.

One of my more favorite people is Peter, a division president that I worked for in Kalamazoo. Peter is a techie turned business manager. I had a direct reporting relationship to Peter and also indirectly reported to four other division presidents.

Usually this is a deadly transformation for the business but Peter understood enough to get by and who to trust. Throughout my career I always dreaded being called into my boss's office because it only meant one thing.

I enjoyed getting called into Peter's office. He was a people person and studied personality traits. More than anyone Peter knew how to diffuse tension and create symbiotic working relationships. Having heard my stories of working with various people, Peter took me on as a challenge. He wanted to rehabilitate me into a kindler and gentler person.

Our conversations always started with, "Richard, there are two kinds of people. One group of people gets ahead in their career because of what they accomplish and the other group gets ahead by making others look bad. The more results you achieve the more you threaten the status quo."

Peter would then go on to say, "Which brings me to another story. Think back to the time of kings and princes. A prince may see a king as old, unwise, incompetent, and about to bring harm to his kingdom. If the prince chooses to challenge the king to a jousting match then he mustn't let him live. You see, if the prince only hurts the king, the king will get up, dust himself off, and tell his knights to behead the prince. However, if the prince does fatal damage to the king he will ascend to the throne. The prince must learn to choose his battles carefully, otherwise constantly annoying the king will result in the prince being beheaded."

I would always thank Peter for the insight and march right off into battle. The first few times though, I had to ask who was the king and who was the prince. It turns out I was always a prince but the king kept changing. In a way, that was a relief, because I was getting paranoid that somebody might be after me. I guess knowing somebody is after you is much better than not knowing.

Camp

As a kid our church held a weeklong camp out at the lake each summer. Unfortunately, I was never able to attend. Either we didn't have the extra money or my parent's were afraid that I'd have a negative influence on proper church-going kids.

It was rumored that there were fun activities like swimming, boating, horseback riding and burning marshmallows. There were battles with rival camps across the lake and ghost stories about some unfortunate soul ritualistically beheaded who now haunts the camp. My friends even spoke of romantic trysts in canoes in the middle of the lake. In the end though, they all returned home itchy and it wasn't always from poison ivy.

Today there are more types of camps than you can shake a stick at. There's space camp, aviation camp, cowboy camp, art camp and even virtual camps. Kids can go to a camp to work off baby fat, learn about computers, or repress their alternative lifestyle tendencies.

As a mature, educated, slightly eccentric man trying to recapture the youth that I never had or deserved, I was suddenly struck by the idea of going to camp.

Since all the mainstream camps had restrictions on age, height and mental ability, I was limited in my choices. This was only compounded by the fact that it was mid-winter.

A friend told me of a Canadian alpine club that offered camps to people of all skill levels and sometimes even accepted people with no skill; she suggested they might even let me join one of their camps.

I still hadn't figured out why I had taken an ice-climbing course the previous year when I applied to attend the club's upcoming ice climbing camp. I was surprised, to say the least, to receive an acceptance letter only a few weeks later.

Apparently my friend was right.

The camp was known for climbing world-renowned waterfall ice. The routes had names like Melt Out, Pure Energy, Balfour Wall, Murchison Falls, Bridal Veil, Kitty Hawk, Polar Circus and Weeping Wall.

Being as this was my first camp, and recollecting the horror stories of camps long past, I was determined not to be the subject of pranks by my fellow campers. They weren't going to catch me off guard, whether it be short-sheeting the bed or a hand in the pot of warm water.

My wife made me promise not to be too much of a negative influence on the other campers and to obey the counselors. She also encouraged me to wear clean underwear, "just in case you have an accident."

There were 11 of us in all, ranging in age from 31 to 48. We were a rag tag group of campers, from short and stout to tall and lanky. There were healthcare workers, salesmen, and accountants. We even had a slew of lawyers available to sue anyone on a moment's notice or even file bankruptcy.

There were four professional mountain guides, world-class ice climbers, who acted as camp counselors. They told us to expect to learn about moving efficiently on ice, placing protection, managing the ropes, avalanche terrain and other hazards of climbing frozen waterfalls. They were always willing to offer words of encouragement. I was regularly complemented, "You swing that axe like a girl" or asked for advice, "What the hell were you thinking?"

We stayed at a rustic hostel. In other words there was no electricity or running water. They kitchen was in a cabin separate from the bunkhouse and the outhouse was a good eighty yard walk. The snow was just below our knees. The temperature occasionally warmed up into the teens a few days.

I quickly learned the true definition of freezing cold during the winter in the Canadian Rockies. Although, this epiphany could have been brought on as a result of my first encounter with a frozen and ice covered toilet seat.

We quickly fell into a pattern whereby each morning we would awake, dress, sprint to the kitchen, complain about the cold, eat breakfast, complain about the cold, clean up, complain about the cold, drive to a trail head, complain about the cold, hike to a waterfall, complain about sweating in the cold, climb, climb a lot, hike back to the car, drive back to the hostel, eat dinner, clean up, sprint to the bunkhouse, complain about the cold, then collapse. It was like heaven on earth.

It was a simple life, yet good, clean and wholesome. Okay, given our group of campers, maybe not clean and wholesome,

Climbing frozen waterfalls we wore crampons, razor sharp spines clamped onto our boots, and ice axes with a razor sharp picks. There are really just a few millimeters of the crampon's front-points and the picks of the ice axe that extend into the ice. Experience ice climbers move like Spiderman, only much slower. Their body is pressed against the ice, they kick their boots against the ice to gain purchase and then set their axes either gently hooking into gaps or by hammering. Good ice climbers make it look so easy and graceful.

I make it look hard and painful.

On the last day, a guide took two of us to the weeping wall standing at 300 feet high frozen and an 85-degree angle. Climbers come from all over the world to climb this beast. I was prepared to leave it for them.

During the first pitch, or rope length, the lead climber broke small ice chunks free and showering them down upon me. A golf-ball sized piece struck my helmet and the noise seemed to echo for quite a while. During the second pitch, a softball size chunk of ice broke and fell 100 feet, glancing off my helmet and striking my shoulder.

On the fourth and final pitch my foot slipped and I lost balance, causing me to fall. The leader was anchored into the ice and rock above me to protect my fall but the rope was at such an angle that I swung like a pendulum as my body struck hard against the ice. Somehow, at the point of impact, my right foot was behind my left calf. The crampon's front-point instantaneously drove through my calf muscle, leaving nothing more than a pin size hole in my pant leg.

Just as quickly, I regained my composure, well sort of anyway, and finished the climb. It wasn't pretty but I had managed to climb the Weeping Wall. My clothes were drenched in sweat and I was completely exhausted.

We rappelled the four pitches to the base of the waterfall, collected our gear and unceremoniously said our goodbyes, "See you at camp again next year."

A few hours later, after the adrenaline ebbed away, I noticed a telltale red spot on my pant leg that revealed a gash in my calf muscle. After making my way to the town of Banff, I stopped by the Doctor's office. The nurse remembered me from my visit the prior winter and took me right into the examination room.

As I lay on my stomach, my pants on the floor, the doctor stitched up my ice-climbing souvenir. I couldn't help but think that it sure was a good thing I wore clean underwear. At least I thought they were still clean.

When I was getting ready to leave the nurse asked when I'd be back in the area again, so she could make sure and fit me into the doctor's schedule. Well, only in Canada can you find that level of service.

Bolivia - A Hungry Animal Hunts

In mountaineering circles it has been said that people who experience the constant success of summiting mountains become complacent and that people who don't experience such success try that much harder. Their overriding need causes them to keep trying until they finally succeed. The feeling is compared to a hungry animal that hunts until its hunger is satisfied, or, I suppose, a bigger animal eats it. I've also heard that, "Once you fall off a horse, you've got to get right back on." I'm not sure who the mastermind was for these bright ideas but they've almost gotten me killed on more than one occasion.

Luckily, I never have to worry about becoming complacent. When certain failure looms on the horizon, a wise person quickly revises their goals to coincide with precisely what they've already accomplished. A mountaineer who has lost all his fingers and toes to frostbite, gone snow blind, and is still a hundred feet below the summit can confidently stand his ground and exclaim, "When I set out to climb this mountain, I only wanted to reach this spot right here. I had no intention of reaching the summit and to think otherwise is ludicrous."

After unsuccessfully reaching the summit of Aconcagua, the highest mountain in the Americas, I somehow decided to undertake a twenty-day expedition to Bolivia's Cordillera Real. They are big mountains in a desolate place that offer the additional challenges of a remote third-world country.

The Spanish named these mountains of the Andes, Cordilleras, meaning knotted ropes, to depict their wild and rugged nature. Although they could easily have been named that because after drinking the water their intestines felt like knotted ropes. The Cordillera Real is Bolivia's foremost climbing region with eight peaks rising above 19,500 feet (6,000 meters).

Of course, no trip of mine is exempt from physical injury. In preparation for this trip, and to avoid having any incidents while in Bolivia, I acquired my injuries prior to leaving home. This also served to provide me with something to do while locked away in my tent for 12 hours a day.

During a family vacation to Canada, three weeks before heading off to Bolivia, my family and I were going to take a tour of a glacier in a 6-wheel drive bus. On the way to get tickets I stopped to take a photograph and slipped on a stair step. We had to drive four hours to reach the nearest hospital where I learned that I had damaged the ligaments in my right ankle and knee. I had a swollen and blackened foot and had to hobble around on crutches, wearing an ankle brace, for the duration of our vacation.

Determined not to let it ruin our vacation we went horseback riding, took a three-mile hike in the mountains, and fished. I honestly began to think that climbing in Bolivia would be less physically demanding. Eventually my wife tired of my grousing after each outing and decided to take matters into her own hands. Since she was driving, we went to the Calgary Stampede rodeo, an outdoor Shakespearean play, a dinner theater, and lots of shopping. Did I mention lots of shopping? By comparison, Bolivia would be a cakewalk.

The downside of pre-paying for the Bolivia trip is that I felt absolutely compelled to go. Besides, I'm too cheap to let the money go to waste. I spent the next two weeks rehabilitating my ankle and hoping all would be okay.

Getting my injury out of the way prior to the expedition would be a good thing since there are no rescue systems in place for the Bolivian outback. There are no helicopter evacuations and the nearest hospital is a full day's travel.

La Paz, Bolivia's most populated city, has an airport at 13,000 feet above sea level, the highest in the world. The U.S. State Department recommends taking Diamox, a drug that aids acclimatization, just to visit the city.

Bolivia is a landlocked country that is slightly less than three times the size of Montana. The terrain varies, from the rugged Andes Mountains with a highland plateau (Altiplano) to rolling hills and lowland plains of the Amazon Basin.

Named after independence fighter Simon BOLIVAR, the country broke away from Spanish rule in 1825. Much of its subsequent history has consisted of a series of nearly 200 coups and counter-coups. Comparatively democratic civilian rule was established in the 1980s, but leaders have faced difficult problems of deep-seated poverty, social unrest, and drug production.

The current goals of the Bolivian government include attracting foreign investment, strengthening the educational system, privatizing business and waging an anti-corruption campaign. Maybe we can get them to the U.S. if their efforts succeed.

Bolivia's mountain scenery is spectacular, with colorful Aymara Indians and ancient thought-provoking Inca ruins. It has been called the "Tibet of the New World." Like Tibet, Bolivia has a grand history of civilization. Ruins of the prominent Inca and Aymara empires still stand, and many people follow the lessons in farming and ranching developed and taught by their ancestors hundreds of years ago. Although, many of the indigenous population have given up farming in favor of the easy money from tourism.

La Paz is situated in a bowl shaped valley. On one side are the indigenous Aymara Indians, selling local crafts and foods along with U.S. exports, in a kind of country flea market atmosphere. On the other is the Spanish colonial.

La Paz and the Altiplano area remind me of Gallup, New Mexico on its worst day. Adobe houses, run-down businesses, snot-nosed children playing in the streets, and people walking miles out in the middle of desolate nowhere. Personal hygiene is not one of the priorities in Bolivia. Shared eating utensils and drinking glasses by customers of the street vendors is the norm. In looking at the sandal clad feet of the Aymara, it appears that the dirt has formed a protective layer that allows them to endure extreme conditions such as climbing on glaciers or hiking through razor sharp scree.

The Aymara Indians have successfully blended Catholicism with their pagan Pachammama beliefs. Priests often perform the rights associated with the Pachammama, performing rituals to bless automobiles and houses among other things. There are some really gross aspects of the Pachammama though. One involves the use of dried llama fetuses adorned with yarn and placed in a basket atop colorful carved wax and stones designed to bring luck, wealth, health, courage, and wisdom.

Although I don't speak Spanish and had forgotten my translation books at home, I was undeterred from making my way around the city.

After recovering from jet lag, I spent my second day in La Paz searching for topographical maps of the mountains we were going to climb. The only place to get these maps is through the "Instituta Geographica Miltrar," a military office on the other side of the city. I had the address written on a slip of paper and, since I don't speak any Spanish, handed it to the taxi driver. I could detect the improvement in my Spanish as I said, "No habla Espanol," and pointed at the piece of paper. It looked like the directions said the military office was located in the front of a medical school faculty building. Once we got to the right street, it was clear by the way the driver was looking at the addresses he was having difficulty finding the place.

Finally, he stopped the car and pointed to a medical school, one of several in the area. I went into the building, which is reminiscent of a heavily shelled building in war torn Beirut. It was a five-story building with no railings. One false step and I was a cadaver for the medical students. There were mounds of paper and trash littering the floors. The classrooms had desks and some of them even had tops still attached. There were young women in lab coats with their small children in tow. I went outside and walked around the building to the back. There was a huge pile of crumpled desks, filing cabinets, and chalkboards that looked as if they had been tossed out the upper story windows. No luck finding anything that read, "Instituta Geographica Miltrar" though.

I walked next door to the dental building, which looked surprisingly worse than the medical building. I'm guessing that's why everyone's running around with gold teeth. On the first floor there was an old lady in a small room that looked like a tiny pharmacy. I sheepishly proclaimed, "No habla Espanol," and waived my directions in her face. She gave me an odd look and then smiled at me with her bright gold teeth. She pulled out a piece of paper and started drawing on it. I thought, "Finally, I'll get there." When the lines on her directions started intersecting and overlapping one another I felt I would be lost forever. I got so desperate that I started asking her questions in English.

"Is it in this building?"
"Am I very close?"
"How far is it?"

When that didn't work I repeated my questions more slowly and loudly thinking it might help bridge the language barrier. She just smiled at me and handed me her directions.

Back on the street I had an epiphany. If I was looking for a military place, I should ask military people for directions. Stopping to get directions from an armed stranger, when neither of us spoke the other's language, was its own adventure.

I stopped everyone with a machine gun and green fatigues, proclaimed, "No habla Espanol," and waived my directions in their face. They would rattle off directions, I assume, in Spanish. When they finished I would shrug my shoulders and point up and down the street. They would then point in the direction I was supposed to go. I figured my search would be narrowed the first time one of them pointed in the opposite direction. After wandering the street for a half hour or so, I finally had one point in the opposite direction. I looked up to see that I was standing in front of a military hospital. It was a collection of white stucco buildings surrounded by high wall. There was an entrance for vehicles and one for foot traffic. Both were heavily guarded by machinegun toting soldiers.

I walked through the entrance and was immediately stopped by a guard. After proclaiming, "No habla Espanol," and waiving my directions in his face, he asked for identification and I handed him my passport. After carefully inspecting me, two armed guards escorted me to the "Institute Geographica Miltrar."

When I walked into the office there were about 20 people milling around. Based on their attire some were military and some civilian. It looked like something from the 1950's, gray metal desks, chairs, and filing cabinets. I approached a friendly looking woman near the door who I assumed was the receptionist and proclaimed, "No habla Espanol," and waived the directions in her face. She just looked at me and smiled. In the background I heard one of the soldiers with stars on his collar say, "Americano," and "No habla Espanol." The room erupted in laughter.

I said, "mapses por illimani, huayna potosi, pequeno alpamayo," hoping that I just asked for maps. The woman pointed me over to a man dressed in a suit and I repeated my request. He laughed, shook his head that he understood, got up from his desk and left the building.

I was relieved when about 30-minutes later the guy returned. He handed me three maps and pointed back to the woman. After a little more back and forth gesturing on the payment amount, I was back on the street and on my way.

I flagged a taxi to stop and hopped in saying, "Hotel Gloria, Por Favor" and the address "909 Potosi." The driver turned around and gave me a shocked look and said, "No" so I hopped right back out of the Taxi and found another. This time when I got into the Taxi, I proclaimed, "No habla Espanol," and handed him the hotel's brochure and pointed. It worked.

After talking it over with folks back at the hotel, they figured that the first Taxi driver thought I wanted him to take me to Huayna Potosi, the mountain, a days drive from the city. Perhaps I should learn the language or sometime I'll end up getting what I've asked for.

A day later we were caught in a chauffeur's union strike and witnessed some fairly violent acts. It was almost like being home in Montana. Anyone in a car was being attacked and we were stupid enough to try and sneak out of town on the back roads. It was too risky and we had to turn around. Upon returning to the city we were walking along the street and happened upon a mob scene where a car carrying a young mother and her two babies was violently overturned, injuring the occupants. The windows were all broken and blood covered the ground. A crowd of men stood laughing and congratulating each other. The police and military stood by and watched without taking any action.

The following day, once the chauffeur's strike had ended, we drove three hours to the shores of Lake Titicaca, the world's highest navigable lake, at 12,400 feet, which sits on the border of Peru. Since we were headed to Cobacabana, located on one of the many islands in the lake, our van was driven onto a small wooden barge and we got on a 20-foot motorboat with 15 other people for transport to the island.

We spent two days hiking in the hills surrounding the city. We took a three hour boat ride to the "Island of the Sun" in order to trek 10 kilometers along the 14,000 foot ridgeline of the island.

On the return boat ride, the weather started getting rough and I thought our tiny boat would be lost if not for the fearless captain, the Minnow would be lost. Our captain and crew consisted of a 15-year-old boy who steered the outboard motor with his foot while leaning over the side of the boat to watch where we were headed. While out in the middle of the lake, where the islands were just tiny dots on the horizon, the plastic jug holding the gasoline started to leak all over the inside of the wooden boat. I would have been slightly less worried if our captain hadn't been smoking a cigarette. The small, enclosed, cabin quickly filled with gasoline fumes, putting a nice edge on my headache and queasiness. Without missing a beat, our captain wadded up a plastic sandwich bag, that otherwise would have surely been cast into the lake, and stuffed it into the leaking hole of the gasoline jug.

Sleeping at the hotel that evening was fitful and I had vivid hallucinations. My bed kept rocking against two-foot waves all night.

The next morning, after once again crossing the lake in a small boat, we spent the balance of the day winding our way through the mountains, first by SUV and then by foot.

Finally we reached the Cordillera Real. It's a beautiful mountain range covered with snow and glaciers. We established base camp at 15,000 feet.

Our first mountain to climb was Point Austria at 17,350 feet. We departed base camp at 8:30 am, just as the sun was clearing the mountains. The climb is a scramble through snow, rock and scree to reach the summit.

We spent the next day working on the glacier, and renewing our skills on snow and ice. We were finally acclimatized and ready for a bit more technical climbing.

Our next target was to summit both Mt. Tarija at 17,000 feet, and Pequeño Alpamayo at 17,750 feet, on the same day. Pequeño Alpamayo has a spectacular snow pyramid visible from base camp. The approach is multifaceted and challenging, moving over beautiful glaciers, high rocky ridges, and ultimately, ascending a steep snow face to its summit. The sheer beauty and diverse terrain is awesome and is matched by the physical intensity needed to climb it.

We awoke at 2:30 am, and after a breakfast of porridge and last minute tinkering, we started climbing before 3:30 am. The night was pitch black and there were no clouds in the sky. The stars were so bright, like headlights from an automobile. The cloudy details of each galaxy were so clear that they looked almost surreal. We were traveling fast and it took us less than an hour to reach the toe of the glacier. The beams of our headlamps lit only a small area in front of our feet. The dark night and crunchy snow seemed to absorb the light so as not to spoil the view of the stars.

After climbing the steep glacial slope for five hours we reached the col leading to the summit of Mt. Tarija. The last few hours of climbing felt as if I was going to hork up all my internal organs. My legs worked fine but my guts felt as if they were on fire. My back felt as if someone had been beating me with a baseball bat.

Bolivia - A Hungry Animal Hunts

All that remained of the mountain was to climb a 60-degree snow slope to reach the reach the summit, 100 vertical feet away. We stopped for a brief rest before beginning the final push. I looked at the summit. It was so close I could taste it. After an internal debate, which I always seem to lose, I announced that I was going to head back down the mountain. Without further hesitation I struck out to descend from the glacier.

Climbing in remote places, for weeks at a time, one is susceptible to many maladies. There's homesickness causing one to wonder, "What the heck am I doing here?" There's cabin fever from being stashed away in your sleeping bag for 12 or more hours a day. Sometimes the altitude is too much for the body to bear and just wears down your resistance.

Even though a casual observer to my life, such as all my family and friends, wouldn't believe it, my personal rule is safety first. The mountain will always be there and as long as I'm alive and well, I can return to climb another day if I want to. Making the decision to descend not only meant that I wouldn't summit but I also knew the expedition was probably going to be over for me.

It took me only about two hours to reach base camp. I climbed into my tent, rolled myself into the sleeping bag and collapsed. As the day progressed, I felt weaker and weaker. I was so nauseous that the mere thought of food or water made me sick. Within a few hours I was running to the restroom, a hole dug in the ground, every half hour. It got to the point that I finally admitted to myself that I was actually sick. When my companions returned later that afternoon, I told them that I needed to descend all the way to La Paz. I thought my problems were due to altitude and was hoping that descending to 13,000 feet would be enough to help to put me right.

One of my teammates had a satellite phone that he was testing for his company and we used it to call for a jeep to pick me up at the trailhead. It took me over three hours to hike down to the trailhead and then two hours driving to reach the highway and another two hours to reach the city. Upon arriving in La Paz we went straight to the hospital. We found one near the U.S. embassy thinking it would be safe, fearing that health care in a third world country would be almost like witchcraft.

The doctor hooked me up to oxygen and prescribed several medications to deal with an infection attacking my stomach, intestines, and kidneys. It felt as if the parasites were growing into some alien creature that would burst from my chest at any moment. My temperature steadily climbed. It was 60 degrees in the city and I was wearing two fleece shirts, a fleece jacket and was freezing cold. The doctor wanted to admit me into the hospital, but a teammate who speaks Spanish, talked him out of it.

I was a little nervous to be back in La Paz because their presidential election didn't produce a winner and was being hotly contested. The second leading candidate is a Coca farmer (i.e., cocaine) who threatened retaliation if he wasn't elected, and the U.S. announced we would cut-off aid to the country if he were elected. I planned to put on my Canadian T-shirt at the earliest opportunity, just in case something happened.

As soon as we reached the hotel, I called my wife, Carrie. She was able to get me on a flight leaving the next morning. I figured that with being in La Paz at an altitude of 13,000 feet my health would improve just getting on a pressurized airplane.

Early the next morning I was whisked off to the airport by one of the vans we had used earlier in the trip, without incident. As the plane flew over the mountains, the sun was just rising and I could see the two jewels that I so badly wanted to climb. Huayna Potosi at 19,974 feet, literally translated as

"Young Riches," is a beautiful and massive glaciated peak that dominates the view as you come in to land at the La Paz airport. Multiple route choices are available ranging from a number of standard routes on the beautiful east face to some of the most challenging and direct routes to be found anywhere in the Andes on the imposing west face. Illimani, at 21,184 feet, is the highest peak in the Cordillera Real and dominates the skyline of La Paz. The glaciated massif is topped by five imposing summits and rimmed with numerous glaciers. The approach travels through some of the most interesting landscapes in Bolivia, to include the Valle de Las Animas, translated as "The Valley of the Spirits".

Back home I learned that my body chose that exact time for my gallbladder to stop functioning. What are the odds of that happening? Even though a surgeon removed it in no time at all, my other organs dearly missed it for about a month. Luckily the gallbladder is like those parts leftover after working on your car. You know it's important or it wouldn't have been part of the original equipment package but as long as everything still runs okay and doesn't rattle too loudly then all is well.

Apparently my ankle wasn't in as good shape as I thought. Not only that but the ailment seemed to have migrated northward, affecting my knee. After the doctor's diagnosis of tendon, ligament, and cartilage damage I focused on the problem and, sure enough, both joints really started to hurt. Having surgery on so many body parts at the same time really helped to build-up my pain threshold. However, at the mere hint of me asking for a scratch or rub sends both my wife and child to the far reaches of the house. I may need to take them to a doctor to have their hearing checked.

With plenty of time on my hands, recuperating offered me the chance to reflect on the beauty and splendor of the mountains and that last glimpse from the airplane window as the sunrise cast a golden light on the snow and rock of the mountain peaks towering into the sky.

    I can't help but think that I'll be back again someday. After all, a hungry animal hunts.

"There may be an end to the journey, but it's the journey that matters in the end."
— Unknown